The Lost Spell
Yismake Worku

Translated by

Bethlehem Attfield

HENNINGHAM
FAMILY
PRESS

First published in 2022 by Henningham Family Press.
130 Sandringham Road, London, E8 2HJ
henninghamfamilypress.co.uk
@HenninghamPress

The right of Yismake Worku to be identified as author of
this work and of Bethlehem Attfield as translator of this
work has been asserted in accordance with the
Copyright, Designs & Patents Act 1988

Printed and bound by Short Run Press, Exeter
& Henningham Family Press, London

ISBN: 9781916218628
ARTISTS' BOOK: henninghamfamilypress.co.uk

Supported using public funding by
**ARTS COUNCIL
ENGLAND**
LOTTERY FUNDED

The Lost Spell

Yismake Worku

Translated by

Bethlehem Attfield

Henningham Family Press
London
MMXXII

Incantation of the magic spells found in this book is not advised; the author will not be held responsible for the consequences.

Foreword

Dr. Admasu Meshesha

Yismake Worku is an Ethiopian novelist who is known for his prolific writing as well as for experimenting with new writing styles. When his bestselling novel *Dertogada* was released, Amharic readers received it with great enchantment. Worku is not the kind of writer who always sticks to one genre just because it is a success. He is set to explore new ways.

The Lost Spell is a result of such exploration. In this book Worku sometimes narrates a single event to what seems like an eternity, and at other times summarizes a whole era in a moment. At times he uses his linguistic skills to present poetic narrations that are breathtaking; at other times he lets his ideas slowly flow like a river.

The precise social, political and cultural critique he outlines at a time when the country was going through political turmoil is witness to his brilliance, as well as his bravery. He relentlessly documents concise facts and undeniable truths; unafraid about consequent reactions from those effected by such public exposure. For those who follow Ethiopian literature, they are unable to tell this era apart from Yismake's literary work. In his novel *Telmid*, he sketches Eastern Ethiopia; in his trilogy *Dertogada, Ramatohara* and *Zantozara* he captures Northern Ethiopia; and now, in this novel *The Lost Spell*, he vividly portrays Southern Ethiopia.

In the past few years, Yismake's written work has caused visible changes in society. His influence is not limited to a growing readership, but also as a role model to other writers who have started to follow his lead. His novel *Dertogada* has stimulated feelings of revival in many disillusioned Ethiopians. While many writers are confronted with writers' block and are unable to string words together, Yismake's prolific writing is a telltale sign that he has an unstoppable imagination.

In my opinion, *The Lost Spell* can be classified as "magic realism." The protagonist, who is a dog, is no ordinary dog. He used to be a human. Didimos Dore undergoes a magical transformation. He starts to explore society's imperfections from a new vantage point. While looking for the magic spell that can return him back to his human form, he gets an opportunity to unveil bizarre realities, and learn about things he failed to do as a human.

The other new technique that Yismake uses in this novel is to weave the history of towns into the plot. For Yismake, towns are not just places but characters in their own right. He manages to show that beyond their faded appearances, towns have vibrant histories. I did not know, until the protagonist passed through the town of Ziway, that the town had such wonderful history. As in his previous works, Yismake sometimes pauses his narration in *The Lost Spell* to reflect, reminisce on and critique ideas and issues at national level. In this book I think he particularly zooms in with full force on the issue of *dehumanization*. He envisions a gruesome world where people lose their humanity and become dogs, and portrays it for us accordingly.

If I said any more I would be spoiling it for the reader. Enjoy your reading!

One

A magic spell has turned me into a dog. If anyone struggles to believe this truth, it's fair enough; even I struggle to believe it. Besides, nobody's belief or disbelief could turn me back from what I have become. If no one cares whether this story is true or not, let them not care. A generation that does not live genuinely, that does not laugh genuinely, that does not cry genuinely, cannot be expected to grasp such a difficult reality.

However, this is the truth of the matter. I, who was created in the image of God, have now suddenly appeared in the image of a dog. I was a human. Lo and behold, I am now a pooch. I am a black mutt to be precise; as black as a burnt clay pot. I have just arrived near a small stream, rippling like a distorted mirror. The reflection shows a dog as dark as the deep night, darker than the curfew hours declared by the government during a state of emergency.

My bloodshot eyes look like the traditional henna-dyed palms of women. My floppy earlobes cover the opening to my eardrums. Yes, my fear is confirmed.

The magic that I have diligently practised since child-hood has not paid off in glamour, instead it has caused this disaster. I never truly believed that it would work. My reckless tampering has led to this muddle. It's confusing, right? Rightly so—I'm confused too. It's shocking, right? Yes, I am trembling with fear.

I am panting, with my long tongue protruding like a hot sword. I am foaming through jagged teeth like ancestral flint tools from Lucy's time; yes the dawn of time, saliva dribbling down my scorched muzzle. What is the verdict then? The distorted reflected image in the stream testifies to my new form—a mutt.

Anyways, where am I? I don't even know where I am. I am in a deep forest adorned with green leafy shrubs. There is no sound other than birds chirping. "Humans?" I think. From now on, what are humans to me? How can I explain that I am (sorry, that I was) a human too? I can't even speak their language. My speech is no longer comprehensible to humans. My fate is to be a dog. I will be considered a dog. I will eat like one and drink like one. Oh, that reminds me; I am thirsty and hungry.

I lean down to the flowing stream. For the first time, I try to drink like a dog. I gulp the water up with my long red tongue but I'm unable to quench my thirst. I actually stir up the sand and make the clear water murky. I wait until the sand settles back down again, then continue my attempts to drink. I imagine chugging the water in one go. What is the use? I can only yearn to become a human again. From now on, being a human will only be a memory. How disastrous! How can a respectable gentleman suddenly find himself turned into a dog? What a cursed day! I have to believe this truth, though it is hard to comprehend. The clothes I had on when I was a human have slipped from my canine form.

You might ask: If you magically turned into a dog, why can't you use magic to turn back to a human? That is what I have been trying to do all day! I can't recall the words to break the magic spell. I never thought the spell would work in the first place. So, you should be asking me: What is it like to be transformed from a man into a dog? My answer may be shocking, scary and may make you tremble with fear....

Who could tell that I am Didimos Dore now? How am I going to enunciate, I AM DIDIMOS DORE? I can only bark now. My lovely wife and children would only see a dog, not me as I once was. My name however remains untainted. If anyone in Addis Ababa asks who Didimos Dore is, he will get a prompt reply. Although no one knows of my hidden tampering with the occult, everybody in my neighbourhood knows of my wealth and status. My father's memory is not yet forgotten.

My father was a famous counsellor to Emperor Haile Selassie. There are numerous records that testify to his reputation as a prominent scholar. He was also fascinated by the prehistoric world. Among a group of archaeologists, between 1943 and 1957, he made significant findings regarding the ancient Axumite kingdom in the northern city of Axum and surrounding area. He undertook his own research into our ancient culture, and made amazing discoveries. Some of the artefacts he found are still displayed in the national museum. He also found several scrolls that he secretly kept at home. He named them the Scrolls of Akilas, after the famous Ethiopian magician Akilas. Before his days came to an end, he passed those scrolls on to me; an heirloom.

I inherited my father's passionate interest and deep involvement in the mysteries of the ancient world. Of my fifty-three years of life, half have been spent in standard education, and the rest in study of the ancient world. I have studied archaeology, philology, and anthropology in renowned institutions in different countries. Even though I have achieved wealth through my hard work, and gained knowledge through my education, my personal fascination with the supernatural has led me astray. The foolish experiments I pursued, to find out whether the spells are real or not, have left me in my present state.

It has been several days since I have seen my wife and children. I miss them. Having become a dog, I miss them more. What can be done? I can't even show them my love. In my mind's eye, I recall the glorious laughter of my fifteen-year-old daughter Eden, which exacerbates my loss. I even miss the sulking of Akilas, my almost eight-year-old son. The image of my wife's beauty blurs before my eyes. Men who pass by my wife often turn their heads and halt like statues. Their ridiculous stance, gazing sideways, reminding me of the lion statue beside the National Theatre. Her smile is as bright as a sunflower. Her laughter makes a long boring day appear lively. Our daughter has taken after her bubbly nature. Until today I was not bad looking either. I know we were evenly matched.

I remember the day I met my wife. Although it was a winter's morning it was bright. The rain that had been pouring all night had finally stopped. As my car had broken down, I left my house and joined the walking commuters. A beautiful lady with generous hips came up from behind and overtook me. She took a couple of steps in front of me and suddenly slipped and fell into a heap. Her short skirt was covered with mud. I quickly helped her get up and gave her my jacket to tie around her waist. She thanked me profusely and told me her name: 'Ephrata'. I extended my hand for a handshake, and said 'I'm Didimos'. From then on we saw each other every day. We had some splendid times. It was when she so hurriedly agreed to marry me that I realised she loved me.

All that is gone! What a desolate day! What a cursed day! How am I going to cuddle my kids now? How am I to kiss my wife? I am a dog, a black dog. Worse luck; my wife hates black dogs. I remember how my wife once rushed with revulsion to the bedroom when she saw a stray black dog that had sneaked in the compound to mate with our dog. Not only that, a few days later we found the same dog lying dead at our front door. I asked her what happened but didn't pay much attention to her reply. Now that I think about it, I'm shocked. When I recall that she hit the dog's head with a club and killed it, whilst its penis was still hanging out of the skin, ready to mate, a shiver passes through me. My son, on the other hand, loves black dogs. I remember how he used to feed some of his food to the same black dog. If I do manage to get home, two contrasting fates may await me; my son's shared meal or my wife's club....

Right! Where am I? In this forest I can't even tell East from West, or North from South. It has been a while since the sun hid behind the tall trees. Oh dear, have I forgotten that I am actually in a forest? Oh really, I should escape! At least I should leave these woods. Which way should I run?

After some hesitation, I flee any which way my legs lead me. For about twenty minutes I run without a stop, shooting outwards like a missile. So far I haven't come to any harm. I can feel hunger pangs, though. What can I eat? I haven't really thought about this before. For the first time I slow down and stop. I look around. It is getting dark. Luckily, I think my vision must have sharpened when I turned into a dog; I can still see. I sniff around for food, but what am I going to eat? Evidently, I should find dog food, not human! Sadly, one can no longer find people who leave bones behind. Addis Ababa's meat eaters chew down bones that even a blow from a lion's paw wouldn't break. They crunch down on them as if they are dried chickpeas, thanking God for giving them molars that can grind bones like a machine.

Every time I think of our bone-loving culture, I recall a particular story. Many years ago, an *Habesha* guy—Abyssinian—went on a scholarship to Moscow. One evening he went out to dine with a Russian friend. He picked up a leg of lamb and started breaking it down with his teeth. He chewed it and swallowed it. The Russian, who had been watching this with surprise, asked my friend: What do dogs eat in your country? Knowing that potatoes are a Russians' favourite food, the Habesha proudly replied "potatoes."

I lean up skyward and start to sniff with my sharp nose. I pick up a smell. Although I haven't planned a route to take, the smell comes from a different direction to the one I am heading. It comes from the left. It is getting dark, but maybe I can find something to curb my hunger, so I head that way. If I don't do something about my hunger I may end up collapsing. If I give in to exhaustion now, getting out of here will become a fantasy. It is inevitable that the forest will be full of dangerous wild animals at night. In my current weak state, I am sure I won't be able to fend off danger. If I suddenly get surrounded by wild animals, I won't have any options apart from putting my tail between my legs and cowering.

As I run with these thoughts in my head, I hear a noise that sounds like an old bugle blaring and I stop in my tracks. I knew it! A hyena. Yes, it is the right time for hyenas. It is twilight for humans and dawn for hyenas. Had I not realised that my time was going with the setting sun? The saying is true: "What is feared will come true, and what is hated will be inherited." I start shaking. I feel my black fur standing on end like a porcupine. Fear is shaking my body as if I am being electrocuted. I stay in the same spot for some time, dancing along to my trembling rhythm until I finally react. I bolt and head to where I picked up the smell.

After a couple of minutes, I find the source of the smell. Oh, Lord of Creation! It is a dying jack donkey. I get closer to take a better look. It is wounded badly. It is moving its tail as if its soul is going to exit through the rear end. I walk around behind it. I was wrong; it is a female donkey.

I start circling around the donkey. Her brown eyes are bulging. The whites of her eyes look like mouldy cheese. I feel sorry for her. Would I eat a donkey? I won't do it. Although I am a dog, I am also human. My body may be that of a dog, but my mind is human. I may look like a dog, but I'm not really one on the inside. What a trial!

Nevertheless, the donkey will get eaten. The hyenas' call is not singing. It is a call to gather and eat the donkey and the noise is increasing in volume. Should I eat her or leave her? What! I am Didimos Dore after all. Would I eat a donkey? I once used to be a respected gentleman, unlike today. I ruminate like this, until I suddenly find I am surrounded by a pack of hyenas. The hyenas cackle as they surround me. This joyless laughter horrifies me.

Two

I don't know where I got the power to break out of the circling hyena pack, but I managed to get away. What amazing power—what energy! How did I break out? I don't recall my steps, but I managed to get away from the hyenas. Evidently, they have no reason to chase me when fortune has provided them with a donkey meal. I imagine how they will tear the donkey apart. Bite, pull, dismember; I can't picture them leaving anything. Once they are done with the donkey, will they come after me? I don't know....

The forest seems endless. I am still shooting outwards like a shuttle charged with unknown power. I know that people have a natural hormone called adrenaline in their body that generates energy. Whatever hormonal kick I had just now, however, is far greater than what helped me jump a wall as tall as Jericho's when I was a young man, or to hold thorny shrubs like flowers.

If I hadn't magically transformed from a man to a dog, I wouldn't have thought so much about a dog's nature. Now I must think about dogs. Although my body, fur to paw, is that of a dog, my mind is still a man's. As a man, I knew a thing or two about the nature of dogs.

I know that a dog's ability to identify grey colour variations is a lot less than a human's. A dog's ability to detect motion is quite sharp. They can tell their owner from nearly a kilometre away. But I am a dog without an owner. I am still traversing the deep forest in total darkness. When I manage to navigate my way, running through the night without crashing against rocks or logs, I realize how sharp a dog's twilight vision is; I can even see insects. Had I been a man, I would have bashed my head ten times, until it ended up looking like a calabash filled with chilli paste. Scientists say that the human field of vision is a semicircle, while dogs (sorry, we dogs) can see three quarters of a circle around ourselves.

We dogs (did I altogether forget that I used to be a man?) have superior hearing to men; we can hear the slightest movement, all the way to ear piercing frequencies. We have four times the ability to hear sounds than man!

Our other great skill, thanks to our moist nose, is our good sense of smell. I can proudly say that our brains are full of olfactory nerves, which detect smell. When

I was a man, I used to admire dogs for this exceptional sniffing skill.

As I still have a human element, the downside of having a great sense of smell is that I suffer from the bad and sickly smells. Although I no longer have the privilege of smelling my wife's delightful fragrance or the natural scent under a baby's neck, I believe I wouldn't pick these up, even from afar, because of the other unavoidable stenches in the air. If someone put himself in my shoes, he would find this sad dog's existence to be so frightening.

The average life expectancy for dogs is about thirteen years. The longest recorded age for a dog is not even thirty years. Longest age indeed!

Is my life to be gauged in dog terms? My age in dog years, my living by dog standards, my performance and rewards on a dog's scale? Do you see my bad luck? I am an old dog. My dog age is over ten years. This means I am over middle-aged. Death's footsteps must be approaching my way.

Oh, for the love of a remedy! Who can get me out of this state? Who do I tell this to, and how? Even if I speak, not that I can; who would be able to use magic to turn me back to a man?

Bluey, famously the oldest dog ever to live, died in 1939 at the age of twenty-nine. So much for being oldest ever! So much for long life! Even the Guinness Book of Records applauded Bluey's long life. But, it also noted that this was unsubstantiated, and that the verified longest age was twenty-six years, for a dog called Pusuke.

My fate is sealed. I will soon be gone. Woe to Didimos! I, who was such a distinguished gentleman, never thought I would die this way. You know, I had so many dreams. Am I to be buried with my dreams? What's to be done? I had it coming! As the saying goes, "A restless finger..."—thus I have joined a world where twenty-nine years of life is *applauded*.

As I run, saddled with my sense of loss, I hear the sound of cars. A bit later I pick out the smell of cattle. I still don't know where I am. Even if I did, what would be the use? I no longer have property, citizenship or kinship; no claim to anything.

I smell people. I have managed to get out of the forest. I feel relief; a weight lifts off my shoulders. I'm going to see people, men, my previous folk! I never thought being merely human could be this enviable. But is it really? Nevertheless, I feel ecstatic to have finally reached a human dwelling without being torn apart by wild animals. At least my life is spared for tonight.

Slowing my pace, I climb up a small hill and look down. I see from afar a fire burning in a small hut. In the other direction there is some kind of road construction or repair work going on. A bit further on, there is some temporary housing for the construction workers. I see a bunch of tin houses. I head that way. I hope to find in this village some leftover food to curb my hunger.

After a couple of minutes, I cross the road and approach the fence of the temporary houses. The people in there are not asleep yet. They talk in English and Chinese and sound like noisy birds.

I get closer to the fence and peep through the gap. Sitting by a fire, the residents are chatting. They are mostly Chinese. There are also two Habesha, and one white lady; I can't tell by her looks where she is from.

As I'm about to go through the fence, a disturbing thought occurs to me. I have heard that Chinese people eat dogs. What if they slaughter me right here and now and enjoy my barbecued flesh? I freeze where I am. Will they barbecue me and eat me along with my dreams? A Chinese guy walks to the fence and fumbles to get his penis, which is as small as a soybean, out. As he is pissing he says: 'A dog!' in accented English. I am unable to move. I freeze. Hoping to eat, am I going to end up eaten? Lord of Creation!

Three

Life has become a slippery, muddy road for me. Without warning, it has slipped me up and changed me from a man to a dog.

For several minutes I stay by the fence and peek through the gap. My hunger is getting worse. I bet I look skinny and shrunken, like a highlander's hat. I can't enter through the fence, but neither can I walk away.

Had I been a determined person (sorry, a determined dog), I would have gone to the small hut with a burning fire and tried my luck. I don't know why I am tempted to get into this compound.

The people who are sitting around the bonfire are all chatting, except the lady. I still can't tell where she is from. Her long golden hair covers her shoulders. Her hair is similar to the flames she stares at. As she turns from side to side, trying to follow the chattering Chinese people, her bright hair swings along. Her blue eyes seem hungry for something. I think she has a habit of nodding her head when she is listening.

She wets her lips with her restless tongue. Being a dog, I am surprised that I can notice and admire a woman's beauty. For a few moments I forget my hunger, as my attention is on her. I wish I hadn't remembered the hunger. I don't know if the hunger is so intense because I am canine. Even if I find food, I don't think I can eat enough to feel content.

Two Chinese men come from behind the houses carrying a whole animal on a spit-rod. A local guy follows with two glittering knives in his hands. He must be the one who slaughtered the animal. His hands are covered with blood. I can't tell if the animal is a dog, a goat, a wild animal or a sheep. The long spit-rod has gone through the neck and come out at the arse. The two men lower the rod onto two Y-shaped sticks, buried in the ground on either side of a fire that burns like a furnace. The head of the animal has been cut off, so I can't tell what it is.

Could it be a dog? I ask myself. It can't be. If it is, I have two sickening worries. The first is, if I get inside the compound, I will be next on the barbecue. I can already imagine the glittering knife on my neck. Oh dear, I do feel sick. I better move on to the second worry. If what is on the barbecue is a dog, and they throw away the leftovers, will I eat them? How on earth could I eat dog meat? I may be a dog now, but my mind is still a man's; an Ethiopian man to be precise. An Ethiopian's conscience would have him running for holy water if he touched a dead body, let alone eating dog meat.

Ever since the Chinese started settling in Ethiopia, I have heard of them slaughtering crows and dogs. It's also known that they enjoy ridiculing us Ethiopians. They say: 'How can you starve when you have so much around you?' Well, that's because it is abominable to eat dog meat. An Ethiopians' gravest vow is: 'If I fail, may God make me eat dog's meat!'

But, according to anthropologists, not only the Chinese but other civilizations, such as the early Romans and Mexicans, are known to have eaten dogs. In modern times, Korea, Vietnam, New Zealand, and a few other Asian countries are known to eat dogs. The fact that butchers and restaurants supply dog meat as a delicacy in these countries is not a secret. Insect delicacies are also not to be overlooked.

Just thinking about these things nauseates me. I must still be Ethiopian in spirit. I should remember that I'm just a dog. Oh damn that spell! This is what happens when one has meagre knowledge. The adage: 'An unwise prayer results in calamity' is right. In the past, unlike today, I never had to think about hunger.

I never even had time to think about the poor and unfortunate. I spent most of my time researching, fascinated by discarded and forgotten ancient knowledge. Questioning if there was truth in our legends and our oral histories. Wondering if there was indeed any truth to the black silk-wrapped secrets of the occult. I will tell you more about my findings later. Right now my aim is just to find a solution to my starvation. I haven't tasted anything since I became a dog.

The barbecue is ready. They move it away from the open fire and put it on a wicker basket. Everybody is given a knife. It is quieter now. They are leaning down with concentration like master-craftsmen, focused on their task—eating. The Habeshas and the white lady are not eating. Could it be because of what I suspect? It doesn't matter. If they do throw me the leftovers, I shouldn't really care what kind of meat it is. I can't really afford to choose what I eat in my pitiful state. In times of starvation, whatever is chewable is food. Even the Bible says that, in times of hunger, people have eaten donkey brain. Nevertheless, during the famines in Emperor Menelik's era, eating a donkey was still frowned upon.

Of the several anecdotes told about the famines, one that took place in Shoa province stands out as the saddest. People brought a lady to King Menelik II for verdict. The lady was pitifully skinny. Her cheekbones were so prominent, and one could count her ribs through her torn clothes. She was brought to justice for having eaten seven children. The King asked her if that was true.

'Yes, I was starving, so I ate them', she replied.

The King was saddened looking at this lady, who didn't seem to have eaten a bite, let alone seven children.

'Oh what tragedy has befallen my country, my people!' The King grieved. The people hastily added:

'Yes, it is unforgivable that she should eat our children, not her own—she deserves to die.'

The King gave his verdict: 'Please show her mercy for my sake. If she didn't have the dilemma of eating your children, she would have eaten her own.'

The accusers obliged and forgave her.

Hunger knows no bounds, dog meat or not. "When one plans to eat a crow, he calls it a guinea fowl." I feel like this saying is so close to coming true. Hunger alters one's reasoning, as does hatred.

Ancient manuscripts record that men in the old days used to eat their enemies. Not only hunger but also hatred makes us eat what we loathe to eat. But the people in front of me are not eating for survival; they are not eating out of hatred either. They are eating meat for the sake of eating.

The Chinese have been eating dog meat for centuries. It is accepted in society as a delicacy. They also believe that dog meat is an effective remedy for many ailments. There is no law in China prohibiting either the selling of dog meat or its consumption. Except, just before the 2008 Beijing Olympics, Chinese animal protection groups started campaigning against eating dog and cat meat. State officials banned the supply of dog and cat meat where the Olympic games were taking place; over a hundred restaurants lost business. But this temporary ban only took place to spare international spectators from seeing dog and cat meat on the menu and being repulsed by Chinese culture.

People call the feeling one gets when faced with new cultures "culture shock." I don't have the time now to name my kind of trauma, the trauma of changing from human to dog, because the Chinese have eaten their fill of what I think is dog meat. Should I go after the leftovers?

If I had the guts to find out what kind of meat it was, I could easily go to the backyard and look for the head. But sometimes the truth is hard to bear. Sometimes we wish that the truth were different, that the facts were not glaringly obvious. There is seldom anything scarier than the truth. I quietly slip through the fence and enter the compound. Everybody's eyes are on me.

The lady gets up and walks to me. The others try to warn her that I might bite her. It looks like she can tell I am not the biting type. I start wagging my tail to confirm that I mean no harm.

She strokes my head. I like it. I feel almost as happy as I would had I been turned back to a man. I wish I could tell her that I am actually a man. I wish that her fingers could have the power of taking my soul out of this black dog's body and putting it back into the man I was.

As if she can tell that I am hungry, she brings all the leftover food and offers it to me. I start to devour it. I slump down on the floor like a soldier preparing to fire a machine gun and attack the bones.

'He must have been very hungry,' she says in English. Not only does she nod her head while she talks, but also while I crunch and crush the bones. The others resume their chitchat. But she still stands, watching me eat up all the bones. She even takes a picture of me. I wonder what I look like eating bones like this? Well, this shows that I am starting to get full.

'My father used to have a dog that looked just like this one. I remember when we were living in Berlin, my father used to stroke the dog first when he came back from his missions, even before he hugged us.' This confirms to me that she is German; she also has a German accent. I don't think the rest of the people are listening to what she is saying.

'Please be careful, don't get too chummy with him. He might have rabies!' says an Ethiopian guy. I am shocked to my core when I realize that I am indeed vulnerable to the rabies virus. I have not been inoculated!

Four

I have spent five days in this compound. The reason I stayed here this long is the hope that my German carer would have me inoculated. I have stayed away from other dogs for fear of contracting the dreadful rabies virus. I went out yesterday evening to look around the surrounding area. I was not on my own; my carer was with me. She has a habit of going to the top of the hill every morning and evening to admire the landscape. I also follow her on her walks and admire nature, sitting next to her. I worry that if she goes to the hill by herself a sex-crazed youth might rape her.

During these outings, the surrounding geographical features help me to figure out precisely where we are. We are in Southern Ethiopia, a rural area just outside Yirgalem town. Yesterday we admired the vista until sunset. She was surprised to see my fascination with the unique natural beauty of the area, as this is a human attribute—not a dog's.

I close my eyes and smell the flowers. I turn my ears to birds singing. I gaze skyward to check out the layering clouds. She follows my gaze and comments in German. Perhaps there is no better language to express her amazement than her mother tongue. I only understand her when she speaks English.

She says: 'Amazing dog!' Then she puts her fingers through the fur on my head and says, 'my sweet, you are beautiful....' My heart quivers with longing for my wife. How can I reply? I only have an inner voice, no ability to vocalize my thoughts.

Germans love their dogs. Even during the Second World War. This lady also seems to have more love and care for dogs than for the many children and infirm people she must see suffering from malnutrition here in East Africa. I know I am exaggerating. It might be wishful thinking on my part; the truth is there is nothing more important to humans than the well-being of their fellows. Everybody values and favours their kind. How about me? Why am I following this lady around instead of finding other dogs to be with? Could it be attraction? I was a man after all, before I became a dog. Maybe it is desire that is making me wag my tail? If it was about finding my kind, why didn't I go to the Habesha? The person I once would have been closest to in race and culture? No, that can't be the reason. It must be because she cared for me. I don't know if it is because of her German background, but she likes me. Even Hitler was a dog lover.

Hitler famously had three dogs called Rolf, Blondie and Bella. He had a school for dogs. The aim of the school was to train dogs to speak German. He hoped dogs would be able to communicate with SS officers, to carry out spying missions and patrols. This shows that Germans believed that dogs had as much skill as humans. German researchers even tried to train dogs to read and write. It might sound weird, or rather ironic, but people like Hitler value dogs more than their own kind.

Some believed that Hitler's dog Rolf could communicate in writing. An honoured woman who heard this story went to see for herself. Rolf wrote on a board: 'My lady, can you wag your tail?'

When Hitler's time was finally up, in 1945, he shot his dog Blondie before he killed himself. Whether he did this out of love or not, we cannot say.

Anyway, the German lady has been looking after me so well. I decided to stay with her not only because of her loving care, but also in the hope that she would get me vaccinated. I really wish she would get me vaccinated. I don't want to die of that merciless rabies virus before my dream is realized. My dream is to be human once more—a man.

Rabies is not the only infection dogs get. There is parvovirus, coronavirus, herpes and others. As most of these other viruses are most likely to affect puppies, I am not as terrified of them as rabies. After all, I am a senior dog.

Rabies is a hydrophobic virus. I am not afraid of water. Dogs infected with the virus chase flies. I haven't been doing that either. My tail is not drooping between my legs. Still, receiving Louis Pasteur's protection seems as remote as the horizon to me. This reminds me of the challenges the famous scientist himself faced.

When Pasteur announced that he had found the vaccine for rabies, nobody believed him. There isn't anything in the world that human beings accept without doubting it first. Most of the prominent findings in the world have faced opposition at first. One day, an old lady shuffled to Pasteur's laboratory. A rabid dog had bitten her son and she was afraid for his life. As she had no other options, she let Louis Pasteur inoculate him. The treatment worked. Until I get that inoculation, I have to be very careful. That is exactly what I did yesterday.

On our way back from hiking, we saw from afar a pack of dogs; mating. Several dogs were flirting with a small-sized bitch. One was biting and scratching his competitor, then returning to his flirting. When a stronger adversary with a boner chased the first, another one would use the chance to mount the bitch. As the pack's entire attention was on her, none of them noticed me. Finally a dog with a shaggy coat, which looked like a worn out blanket, got lucky. While the others fought one another, he mounted the little dog and started humping away. He didn't seem to mind the bites he got from the others. When he got off, another had a go but could not pull out. The two dogs started pulling away in different directions like a car being towed. The others realized they wouldn't have a chance now. That was when they noticed me.

I felt like hiding inside the German lady's skirt, which was being lifted lightly by a gentle wind. The lady was watching the mating with great fascination. Human beings like comparing their behaviours with animals.

When I started to get more attention from the other dogs, I turned around and sprinted. They chased me until I got into the compound. From inside the fence, I growled fiercely at them. The lady also came running and threw stones to chase them away.

Today, I haven't taken a single step out of the compound. The lady has just returned from her evening walk by herself. I don't know how she feels about my staying behind. I have been such a coward. I regret it. This kind of betrayal isn't expected from a human, let alone a loyal dog. I guess it is my human element that made me such a coward, otherwise I should have loyally guarded my carer. What if this beautiful lady was raped in the woods? I'm such a chicken—cluck, cluck, cluck—and selfish.

I don't think Gelly, my carer, holds any grudge against me. She comes towards me. I wag my tail. Is that my apology? She squats down and caresses my head as usual and summons me to her room. She gives me a plate of diced meat. I no longer wonder if it is dog's meat. She also offers me a bowl of water.

When I'm done with my food, she fills a tub full of water and makes it bubble with soap. She tugs me to make me step in. I step in without hesitation, like a person used to bathing. She looks surprised. She then starts pouring water on me to make my fur wet, and brushes it out to get rid of my filth and fleas. She notices that the water has turned brown with muck, so she pours it out and rinses me with clean water. What a blessing, to have found this lady. What would have happened to me if I hadn't had the luck to bump into her?

Yet I am confused when she closes her door and gets into her bed naked. She smiles and summons me to get on the bed. I hop onto the bed without hesitation. Should I have hesitated? I'm confused. Could this be what I think it is? Could it be true? Do some people have sexual intercourse with their dogs! What is she thinking? I don't understand what she wants. She is caressing me. Am I going to go along with this? Lord of Creation! Gelly starts getting excited. She pulls me closer to her neck. Were I still a man my heartbeat would be racing like crazy. This is shocking! I think she has forgotten that I am a dog. But I don't want to disappoint her. I slide my long red tongue on her slender neck. She moans—in ecstasy?

A sexual fixation on non-human animals is called "zoophilia." People who practice this are called zoophilic, or just simply "Zoos." I don't know if Gelly has had such experiences before. What she is doing now is making me wonder if she is a "Zoo." I think a deep psychological study needs to be done to find out why Zoos develop a sexual desire for animals. Everything has a beginning. I can't ask Gelly if she is like that. She thinks I am a dog. I can't speak like humans anyway.

My tongue, palate, larynx and lips are barriers to me producing human sounds.

Anyways, if I were to ask her in a human voice while she is aroused like this, she might lose her mind. After all, she can never have heard a dog talk before. She might even be struck dead; thinking that God was rebuking her through a dog for her sexual deviance. Surely Gelly is now swimming in a sea of arousal. It seems to me like she is swimming in a deep fire of Gomorrah. Her body is on fire. Her face turns red. She arches her back and pushes her plump breasts, close to my face. *Gelly... Gelly?*

I only found out that her name is Gelly the other day. I found out when I heard Chu, one of her colleagues, call her. Crazy Chu always seems to have her name on his lips, just as he always keeps his white eyeglasses on his nose. In his line of work, considering his speed and restlessness, he would have lost his eyes long ago if it hadn't been for the protection of those glasses. I think he even keeps his glasses on when he is asleep. He should indeed keep them on at all times, otherwise the angels of protection will be busy looking after him while the rest of us are neglected. Although Chu is restless and impatient, one can easily sense that he is a bright engineer. His general knowledge is admirable.

He always seems to criticize the Ethiopians that work with him. He often mentions that they have half-baked knowledge and that their appetite for food surpasses their appetite for work a thousandfold. Last night he was lamenting that Ethiopian workmanship is inferior.

'They are shameful! Shame on them.' Chu called out to Gelly sarcastically, imploring her to listen. 'An Ethiopian's work-ethic is the most pathetic in the entire world. You would think that they are being forced into slavery, instead of working for their nation.

'Gelly, you know what? The other day I nearly beat their heads with a spade, like snakes. Their task was to bring wet concrete in a wheelbarrow. When they were picked for the job they promised they would do it efficiently. They did well the first two or three times. Eventually what they put in the wheelbarrow wasn't even a spadeful. I doubt it would weigh a kilogram. To give the impression that they are hard working, they work quietly. When you look at their faces, they look like storm clouds. Their eyes look as red as chilli pepper. They don't have a wristwatch. They often check the sky, as if they can urge the sun to set with their eyes. I follow their eyes and check the sun. It refuses to budge. When I look back, they seem to have been paused by a remote control. I am angry. When they notice that I am heading their way, they start to move as if somebody has pressed the play button.

'This time I walked ahead of them to the concrete mixer, picked up the spade and waited for them. They didn't look alarmed at all. I had evil thoughts then, but I resisted the temptation and quickly dropped the spade, like it was a hot metal rod. I then calmly picked up the spade and doled large quantities of the concrete mixture into their wheelbarrows. They pushed the barrows so slowly. It seemed like they were trying to make the trip last. They took light steps as if the road was made of glass. I wonder if somebody told them that their work does not matter to their nation? Everywhere you go it is the same story.

'If civil servants cared about their work like they cared for their tea break, the system would function efficiently. If you see how they race to leave the office at lunch break, you would think that they were escaping from fire. When they return from their break, they drag their feet as if somebody has chained a rock to them. They treat their clients like enemies. They chide and complain all the time. They think that they are doing the client a favour, instead of carrying out their duties.'

Gelly just listened and made no comment. I think Chu likes Gelly. If she wasn't his manager, I think he would have tried his luck with her. He may still do so. I wonder what he would do, if he saw me giving her such sexual pleasure, merely with my tongue on her neck! He would definitely kill me, and barbecue me for dinner.

I wish Chu did know how Gelly likes me, that she prefers my rough fur to his soft skin. Maybe some people prefer rough blankets to silky bed sheets because of their zoophilic tendencies. Chu should know that his sarcastic gossip means nothing to her, while my incomprehensible bark is music to her ears. Why am I thinking of Chu so much? Could I be scared of him? Well, he should know that I am perfectly capable of sinking my sharp teeth into his throat. But what would happen to Gelly if people found out that she is a Zoo! My life would be in danger and she would be stigmatised!

But don't they know the practice of sexual inter-course with animals has existed since ancient times? In Italy, researchers from Cambridge University found cave paintings of people in acts of bestiality that date back ten thousand years! Nobody knows if what these cave paintings depict reality or imagination. But it does show this practice is not new.

Oral histories also reveal that Zoophilia is as old as the hills. There is a strange folklore that relates to the creation of silkworms in Korea. In a time of grave national crisis, the King's daughter tried to come up with a solution. She made an oath that if the crisis came to an end she would marry a white horse. The crisis indeed came to an end and the princess kept her word by marrying a white horse. She begat a silkworm from the horse. That is why the silkworm is as white as the snow.

Ancient Egyptians, Greeks, North Americans and Middle Eastern people all have this tradition of inter-course with animals. In the middle ages, European priests were taken to court for the same practice.

Well, this experience is certainly bringing back everything I have read and heard about zoophilia! Recently, it was in the news that an Indian woman had publicly married a dog. There were over a hundred guests celebrating their union! In an interview she said that she had no regrets about marrying a dog. About twenty years ago another Indian lady married a huge python in a public ceremony.

That same year, a Sudanese man was taken to the village elders for having sexual intercourse with his neighbour's goat. The elder's verdict was for the man to pay a penalty of fifteen thousand Sudanese dinar and marry the goat.

On the other hand, Gelly, some countries will punish bestiality by law. Ethiopian penal law clearly states that it is a criminal offence, although I don't know of anyone who committed this act. But the law says any person engaged in a sexual act with an animal shall be sent to prison.

Oh Gelly! It is also condemned by God. How could I forget, the Bible strictly forbids it. Leviticus 18:23 states, "A man must not defile himself by having sex with an animal. And, a woman must not offer herself to a male animal to have intercourse with it. This is a perverse act." This points out two facts. First, that sexual intercourse with animals existed in biblical times, otherwise they would not have needed to come up with the law. Second, that women as well as men were known to have engaged in these acts. The Gentiles cast out by God all defiled themselves in this way. The Assyrians, Phoenicians and the Chaldeans were reputed to engage in bestiality.

Yet, from a health perspective, there is no evidence that her desires will lead to health problems. Except the claim that HIV/AIDS originated from monkeys. I don't think they did an HIV/AIDS test on the monkey in question, though. I believe this was a lie to avoid inquiry into its true origins, and the virus was fabricated in a laboratory. The West wanted to say it originated in the Dark Continent, Africa.

There should be an in-depth, scientific, cross-sectional study into these desires involving Psychology, Zoology and Zoo-anthropology. The feelings that animals have towards humans should be rigorously studied. I may be the perfect candidate for these experiments! Dogs know their fellow dogs best. One needs to be in these shoes to understand how it feels.

I am not entirely a dog, though. I am half-dog, half-human. I am a dog that feels and thinks like a human. But, right now, I am altogether confused. My tongue seems to have it's own free will over Gelly's body. If a man's need for food is satisfied (sorry I mean, if a dog's need for food is satisfied) the next natural desire is sure to follow. Unless this is controlled by some great moral discipline, the need is inescapable. The saying: "The craziness of a monk and the politeness of a dog are uncharacteristic" suddenly comes to my mind. I watch my red penis sliding out like a lipstick from its black furry sheath. Oh, Lord of Creation! Although I am a dog, I am also a married man! The image of my beautiful wife momentarily blocks this vision of Gelly. While I am being torn apart with hesitation, a creaking sound makes me turn to the door. Chu comes into the room, closing the door behind him. I think: This will be the end of me.

But Chu does not even look at me—as if nothing is happening at all. He only has eyes for Gelly.

Five

I spend the next few days feeling remorseful over my dishonourable behaviour, and indecisive about what I should be doing next. I feel like I have to go back to my home.

My beautiful wife shouldn't suffer loneliness any longer. My children must also be missing me. All they know is that one day their father left in his car and never returned. It has been months. They may even think that I am dead.

I hate to think my family may conclude that I am dead. In that case, my children will have grieved and got used to life without me. My wife may have married another man. Oh no! My wife is beautiful! She normally gets a lot of unwanted interest from other men, even when I am with her. I sometimes used to feel jealous, and at other times proud over the attention she got. I don't want to hear that my wife remarried thinking that I am dead. I want this to stay a worry and not become a reality.

Whenever this worry starts to get intense, I feel like fleeing towards my home. If my house wasn't so far I would leave right now. It is so far away, especially considering that I have to travel on foot. I try to calculate how many days it would take me. Just thinking about it tires me. There is no point in trying to find my car first. I am a dog now; a creature trapped in an unthinkable position. This being the reality of my broken life, I won't be able to drive my car like dogs do in cartoons.

Life is not a make-believe world, like animated movies, where drawn figures are brought to life with colours and carry out heroic deeds. In the real world one needs legs to walk; a neck to turn. One needs freedom of choice to make decisions, the ability to drive, and one needs a foot to use the brake.

I wonder if my car is still where I left it? I don't think so. I recall parking my car and walking into the woods to carry out the magic ritual. The Maraga forest is on the road that runs from Yirgalem, through Dilla, to Moyale and the Kenyan border. I know I left the keys in the car. Maybe some lucky guy found the keys and got away with the car. Or maybe my wife reported me missing and the car is being held as evidence, or has been given back to my wife.

Anyways, I won't need the car unless I manage to turn back into a human. If I can't drive it, it is as good as a calabash to me. Talking about calabash reminds me of the ancient philosopher Diogenes. He lived in a small tent with no possessions other than a walking stick, a calabash and a dog. One day he saw a shepherd drinking from a river, using his hands to scoop the water. So, he realized that the calabash was surplus to his needs and he threw it away. I feel proud that the dog was essential to the Philosopher. Rightly so! To be one of the philosopher's three essential worldly goods is not a small matter. Although his motto seems to be: "One who has a lot has not profited, one who has little is not in want", I personally think the saying: "The servant lives by his hands, the dog by its nose," works better here.

When I was a man I had high hopes for the oil that was being explored in Ogaden. A promising prospect to haul our nation out of poverty. I used to watch TV news, not for the political propaganda that is commonly aired, but hoping to hear news of success at Ogaden's oilfields. Now that I am a dog, a potsherd of milk is more valuable to me than a barrel of oil. The bottom line is; my car is of no use to me now. I have to face the long journey on my paws.

The journey is fine—I can do it, but what about the inoculation? I am bound to meet other dogs on the way. This means I inevitably face a fight, but what about rabies infection? I can handle dogs, but I am afraid of the virus. Even when I was a human, it was a person's attitude that I got to like or dislike, rather than the people themselves. This is not the time to reflect on what my identity, my beliefs, my values were, back when I was a man. I have many dreams (apologies, I keep forgetting that I am a dog—I had many dreams) I don't want to die with unfulfilled dreams. It is unfortunate to die with unfulfilled dreams. I need to turn back into a man to fulfil these dreams. My hope is that I will manage to turn back into a human. There is nothing greater than hope. A man without hope and a crow without wings are alike. They both can't go anywhere. For someone who had been a human before, it is preferable to die than live as a dog. Of course, if a man cannot live upright—if a man lives on the surface like a man but acts like a dog—then that is a disgrace. It is preferable to be like me; a dog on the outside but a man on the inside.

When I was human I was Ethiopian. I wasn't presented with this citizenship; I was born with it, through the very blood that pulsed through me. My very own folk—humans who wagged their tails like dogs, who sold their dignity for scraps—they've tried to degrade me to the status of a dog before. But I burn like a furnace when somebody dishonours my national flag, let alone my dignity, so I never let them succeed. Yes, I still have hope. I have hope that I will turn back into a human. Life is dreadful without hope.

I did not stay all these months because I was captivated by Gelly's body; it was the hope of getting vaccinated. But it doesn't seem to have occurred to her at all. She may have assumed that I am already vaccinated, or that I am just healthy. The road construction project seems to be coming to an end, so Gelly may be leaving soon. Chu may still be holding a grudge against me; at the end of the project he might eat me.

Though he saw me flirt with Gelly, he didn't react as much as I feared he would. Back then, when he saw me lick her for the first time, he just placed the papers he had brought on the table and left as though there was nothing unusual going on. I was ready for an attack, thinking he would act as any Habesha would, but he hasn't been violent towards me so far.

However, even though he is not an Habesha he might be jealous, as any man would be. I wish he knew I am not besotted with Gelly's body anyway. If it hadn't been

for the hope of inoculation I would have left long ago;
the very reason I'm being indecisive about leaving.

Although my mind is gripped with several anxieties,
the hope of turning back into a human is still most
prominent in my thoughts. An idea suddenly flashes
into my mind. Why don't I put being a dog to good use,
until I become human again? I try to philosophize:
"We have to use what we are, until we become what we
wish to be." Make the best of what we are. It is easy if
you think about it. What would I do if I were a leader?
What would I do if I were a prisoner? What would I do
if I were a beggar? In the same way, it should be easy to
imagine what I would do if I were a dog. I am already a
dog, but I have to think from a human perspective. If I
was given the chance to be a dog, what good use could
I do with it?

I could be a spy! A 'spy dog.' I could easily access
information as a dog that I wouldn't otherwise get as
human. I used to have a knack for unearthing secrets
when I was young. Yes, from now on I will spy. I can put
the outcome of my spying to good use when I become
a man. I will investigate the country's state of affairs
from all the sources I can find. Who will suspect me?
If I spied from Ogaden desert to the highlands of the
North; from common village talk to the palace in Arat

Kilo? Nobody would. I am a dog, after all. So; I have made up my mind to become a spying dog.

Six

I am about to start my spying—the "spying dog." The saying "information is wealth" is true. As it is the age of information, everybody wants information; from the trader to the burglar, from the leader to the follower, from the researcher to the investigator, from the gambler to the bartender.

The trader needs information, not only to find out what to buy and sell, but also to know when to buy and sell. It is obvious that many business tycoons use international spies for commercial espionage. To be a competitive entrepreneur it is essential to use professional analysts who can predict profitability of investments in the long run, using past data. European and Asian companies have put in place countless informants to spy on African commerce. There are trade spies in Ethiopia whose job it is to find out seemingly trivial data, such as the average local shoe size.

Our political leaders have also sent out their 'information-thirst-quenching spies' to every corner of the country. Their ever-present secret agents greedily load their info-pouch with all types of news, to answer the inevitable question their bosses pose: "What did the public say today?" The information collected from gambling houses and bars or any walks of life, depending on the nature of the topic, will be analysed to gauge the public psyche.

Gamblers spy on the cards of their opponents. The local brewer sends a taster to see if her neighbour's beer is better than hers. If the taster is drunk and never returns to report to her, she will know to make her brew stronger. If she can't win the competition by improving her beer's quality, then she will send out false news to discredit her competitor and get her out of business. Something like, "a toad was found swimming in the beer she serves," will do just fine.

Anyways, as this is an information age, anyone who ventures out without information is like a blind person who walks without a guide. The blind person will either end up falling off a cliff, or banging themselves against a wall. So, using what I am—a dog—for spying purposes, is justifiable.

I am ready to snatch away any information I would have been unable to get as a human. The same way our leaders are spying on us, the public, the public will have a chance to spy on the leaders through me. There is no such thing as trivial information.

Imagine having the opportunity of spying in the presidential palace. As a dog, my chances of sneaking through the fence are high. I am sure the guards would be looking out for people, not dogs. Even the special security forces would need divine intervention to tell that I was once a respectable man, now turned black dog.

I would go past the palace fence like any other dog would. I remember the fence is made of metal grills bearing the engraved initials of Emperor Haile Selassie the First. Every time I passed by the palace in my human days, I used to take a peek inside without fail. What I don't particularly recall is; how big the gap between the metal bars was. This will have to be something I see when I get there. It will be easy for me if the gaps are wide enough for a dog to squeeze in. If not, I may have to slip through the gate, using the high officials' luxury cars as cover. What if a bullet from a special security force officer cuts my life short? Well, I need to make this plan work at any cost. Spying requires great discipline and a winner's frame of mind. It requires stamina as well as the willingness to give up one's life.

I am willing to dedicate both, because I am running out of time. I am now counting my life in dog years. If I don't turn back to a human soon—my death is getting nearer moment by moment. But, I can't recall the spell to reverse me back to a human. I can only recall two useless words.

The first few days after I turned into a dog, I tried so hard to recall the reverse spell. But my effort was in vain, just as a woman who goes into labour without being pregnant labours in vain. On the verge of hope-lessness, my efforts to find a means of reversing my situation diminished and I started to gradually accept my "dog" state. Accepting one's identity is inescapable. I am a dog. I am a dog. I am a dog, and I am not going to waste this opportunity. Accepting one's identity is not enough. One should use the opportunity presented by identity to beneficial use.

It is appropriate that I consider my present condition and decide to become a "spying dog." My decision to start spying on the Presidential palace in Arat Kilo is also good. Instructions are always issued from the top and carried out down the chain of command. Although the lower ranks are the reflection of the top, the foot-steps are of the higher command. The footsteps are recognizable. The size is large; on the higher side. It requires meticulous care to study the higher ones. As the saying goes, "fish starts to get foul from the head"— to identify well-being, one needs to start sniffing at the head. The rest of the body is at the mercy of the head, as we all are. Ultimately, there is no creature better at sniffing than dogs.

I will get there. I will go to Arat Kilo. I have heard that there are about twenty dogs in the palace. I hear they all belong to the Prime Minister's wife. If my sources are correct, foreign dignitaries gave these dogs to her and they are kept very well. They have fancy lives, they are regularly shampooed and perfumed.

I am envious. That is not unusual though; even people say of the rich, "I wish I was his or her dog." I bet the security guard who guards the palace feels the same way. Who would blame him if he does? Imagine this contrasting scene; the guard's fingers freezing from frost at night, while the First Lady's dogs lazily wag their tails to show their bliss.

I used to think that, leading a country where several children die of hunger every day would be a nightmare. I never guessed that such badly needed state resources could be used for the upkeep of twenty pets.

This reminds me of the last Emperor of Ethiopia, Haile Selassie, who lived in the very same palace some forty years ago.

The King had a small Japanese breed of dog, called Lulu. Lulu was such a privileged dog, even allowed to sleep on the King's bed. Lulu was so close to the King that they seemed to have a special ability to communicate with each other. The King designated the special duty of belittling overreaching royal ministers to Lulu. As if the King had whispered to Lulu to "go and show that greedy official his place," the dog would run and pee on the official's shoes.

The Minister could not appear offended or chase the dog away. The consequences would have been unimaginable if he did. Once the psychological humiliation was achieved, the rest was easy. There appeared a servant whose duty it was to clean the mess from the unfortunate minister's shoes. His role was as important as the minister's, because the servant doubled as a spy; listening to what was said under the minister's breath while cleaning the shoes and reporting back directly to the King.

I have no idea if the twenty dogs now at the palace have any special duties. I may be able to find out if I get lucky and join them. To be honest, I don't think I will be one of them. I am not that lucky. They say: "If not heaven, then hope for a fitting damnation". Similarly, in my case I can say: 'If not the palace lounge, then wish to squeeze through the fence'.

While the relationship between leaders and their dogs seems good in our country, the opposite is true with the President of Comoros. Ali Solih is known for having ordered a special squad to exterminate all dogs on his island. I believe this cruel act should have been tried in the Hague International Court of Law as genocide. I must admit I didn't consider this a tragedy when I was a human. How could I? Living in Africa, where the lives of multitudes are destroyed as insignificantly as weeds, it would be considered absurd to have an outcry about the extermination of dogs. On the other hand, dogs would cry out. When we see dogs leaning up skyward and crying out, *Woooohoooo,* maybe they are telling God of their grievances about their fellows in Comoros.

Let me recall the story. Ali Soleh was sleeping on a bed that seemed as big as an island. A nightmare made him toss and turn in the huge bed. In this frenzied dream a man, escorted by a fierce dog, was chasing the

President. The President woke up with a start, just as the dog was about to tear into his leg muscles with its sharp teeth.

When the President realized that this was a dream, he poured himself a glass of brandy and decided he would pass a decree. The following day, a decree commanding the extermination of all dogs on the island was issued. On the same day, a special squad was sent out to oversee the extermination of hundreds of dogs. Oh Africa; how many fools are going to make a fool of you? These fools look superhuman in their expensive suits. They think there is no one wiser than they are, and we hope they are right. The dogs of Comoros however learned otherwise; they found out that their leaders are empty inside.

I made a quick prayer, a dog's prayer, for our President not to dream of dogs chasing him. If he had such a dream, it would be the end of us dogs. It would be inevitable, considering his record for passing decrees aimed at a single enemy. He even pretends that these decrees were passed through parliament to make them seem legitimate. It is also rumoured that he has done this to his comrades in arms. Whatever the case, I am still determined to head to the palace in Arat Kilo. The day that I must say farewell to Gelly is getting nearer.

Seven

For the last time, I take a good look at Gelly. If I weren't a dog I would be getting teary. I can't imagine what she would feel if she knew that this is my goodbye. Perhaps her blue eyes would be awash with tears. I don't know, but it is not that difficult to guess that she wouldn't want me to leave. Anyways, nothing can stop me now from my intended journey to Addis Ababa and into the palace; not even Gelly.

When I was a man, Tilahun Gesesse's song: "Break-ups are like death for those who are in love," used to make me feel sad. If I were able to speak and sing right now, I would sing that song. I didn't realize until now that the thought of leaving was so huge a burden. It weighs down my soul. It makes my Achilles tendons tremble like a strummed string instrument. It wrenches my dog heart. Is the idea of leaving harder because I am a dog?

I went through separations many times in my previous life. However, I don't think I ever felt it this deeply, not even when I left my human life and became a dog.

Separation is ripping me apart. It ripped me from the realm of humankind. It is now ripping me from Gelly. I can't take my eyes off Gelly's eyes. We keep staring at each other's eyes, as if our gazes are glued together. They can't be glued though, because her eyes are blinking as fast as usual, even while holding my gaze.

Gelly is sitting on a stool and tanning herself in the morning sun, in the compound. I hope she has not taken the Greek epithet for us Ethiopians—"burnt face"—literally, and is trying to become like us.

Gelly is not so shallow. Apart from being a good Engineer, she is a well-read person. So I am sure she knows of the Greek myth that relates how an Ethiopian, passing by the sun in his spaceship, got burnt and dark, and takes it for what it is—a myth.

Oh, what a great reputation we used to have, once. Sadly our good start has been put on hold, or worse; we seem to regress by the day. Not only has our nation shrunk in size, but also our people's mentality seems to have shrunk down with it. We don't have dreams or visions. Just as waves bedevil a discarded boat, profiteers are messing Ethiopia about. Just as leaves, not of their own will, are carried away by the wind; Ethiopia also does not have Her own will. The passer-by clears Her paths. Traitors stamp out Her footsteps.

Everybody wants to feed Her their own ideology, until She is unable to swallow any more. A child has the ability to puke, but our country doesn't have the strength. Just like a starving cow, one can lead Her to any pasture one desires, not the field She would prefer. She does not even have the strength to regurgitate the cud. She hopelessly waits for the undigested food in Her gut to blow up and kill Her. If She were at least able to belch, it would ease Her discomfort, until some other herder forces Her to eat from another undesirable pasture. While the herders handed Her over from one to the other, the Creator remained faithful to Her and refused to hand Her over to any other gods. While I am thinking about this, I take my eyes off Gelly and look down, as though I'll find the Creator on the ground. Instead of the Creator, my eyes find a torn newspaper. Maybe the other part was used as toilet paper.

The newspaper looks weathered. It will get crispy dry by around noon and the wind may blow it away, to pieces. Even if it survives the weather, I doubt anyone will get to read it.

It is rare to see an Ethiopian reading. Ethiopians are known for draping their traditional scarfs. They start to feel the cold when they read, but when they drape their scarfs they feel warm. They seem to care more about their skin than the state of their brain. The habit of listening a little and talking much is abundant, while reading a lot and saying little—learning a lot and passing on the knowledge—seems to be fading.

The fate of the torn newspaper is either to end up in the toilet or to be used for cleaning windows. Newspapers are more often used for cleaning windows than enriching the mind.

I make out the words in the worn-out newspaper. Shocking news! Although the paper is torn in two, like our nation, I can still decipher the message. It is about political prisoners who have been handed down heavy sentences. It states who has been given long-term imprisonment, and who has been given a death sentence. It also seems to go further than informing us of the news, and goes on to predict future outcomes. I find the predictions more shocking than the news. It says that if the political prisoners ask for pardon, then the government may consider it. This is the first time the word "pardon" ever shocked me. It sounds like mockery to me. How long are we to be mocked like this? Although the idea of a pardon is noble, it is repulsive when it is used to make fools of the public. How long are we to be force-fed with such a heady brew? What mockery of such a noble idea!

Is anyone ever going to genuinely represent this country? Genuinely be ostracized for his or her beliefs? Genuinely be persecuted for this country? I am angry. If I weren't a dog I would hurl insults. If someone wants to struggle for his beliefs, let him struggle; if not, let him hold to his own thoughts. But please don't make a mockery of us with these counterfeit terms adopted by confidence tricksters. Who is going to go to prison for his country, like Mandela did for more than two decades? How long are we to be mocked by those who would release Barabbas and persecute Jesus?

I recall the faces of some of these political prisoners. Never, I think to myself, would I wish for these amazing intellectuals to be imprisoned, even for an hour, but I do not wish for them to be released with this "forged pardon" either. They should not be a part of this drama, and allow this generation to end up being mere spectators.

How long are our politicians going to be profiteers? How long is the public to swallow their fraudulent news? I grind my teeth. Then I pick up the offending newspaper, chew it to pieces and spit it out. Gelly is watching me, wide-eyed. "Oh my God! You can read? Ha!" she says. I think she even understands that I am upset about what I have read. I can't answer her. I can't talk. Well, this is as good a time as any to leave! I think. I look at her for the last time and sprint out of the compound.

Having made a good distance, I can't resist turning around for one more look. I should turn into a pillar of salt like Lot's wife.

She is running after me. I know she won't catch up; I have gone quite a distance. My journey to Addis Ababa has begun. I fly like a ball struck by a golf club.

Five kilometres into my journey, I pass the town of Yirgalem on the left and pause before turning right. I think of going into the town and finding some scraps to eat. If I don't eat, I won't have the strength to get to the capital.

Eight

I wander around the entire town. I am still quite choosy about what I eat. I could have eaten a few things if I hadn't turned my nose up at them. I saw a goat's head being thrown out from a small butcher's. A puppy came out of nowhere and grabbed it before it reached the ground and ran away.

I am now sitting in front of another butcher's shop, eyeing greedily what is on display. I notice the spelling error on the sign above the shop. I don't find it funny. For the residents of this town, Amharic is not their first language. The sign that reads "Meat House" also has an illustration of a slaughtered bull hanging down. The bull still has its head. Usually the bull is hung up after being slaughtered, so you don't expect to see its head. I guess the artist did that on purpose because, if it wasn't for the horn and the hump, the animal could have looked like a dog.

The butcher stares at me and he sharpens his knife, like he wants to slaughter me. If I hadn't arrived late in the day, the queue to buy meat would have blocked my view.

I don't think this butcher is going to throw any scraps for me. I have seen several pieces that he could have thrown to me. The meanness of people knows no bounds. I have seen several pieces he cut that he could not possibly sell or make any use of. I'd better move on.

How can I not find something to eat in this town? How am I going to make it to Addis Ababa? I decide to make one more round of the town before I give up. I go past several hotels and butcher's. I finally get lucky while walking past a house where an old lady lives. She throws me a piece of meat that resembles a miserable old shoe. She curses aloud as she throws the meat away.

'Why can't I buy what I want with my own money? Do I need to be a wealthy merchant to be able to buy good meat? I can't possibly eat this. Here, I doubt if a dog would eat it!'

I feel sorry for the old lady. She watches me eat the meat, as though she regrets throwing it away in the first place.

I resume my journey. Now that I am no longer hungry, I start to notice the beauty of the town. Ras Desta

Damtew founded the town about ninety years ago, but there has not been much progress down the years.

The stones that are put on top of the houses' tin roofs are testimony to how old and neglected the town is. The poet Debebe Seifu was born and raised in this town. I still remember a few of his golden verses, dedicated to this town, *Yirgalem*:

> *Oh......Yirgalem*
> *Colour of my childhood dream;*
> *The ray that made my eyes open*
> *Over that golden horizon.*
>
> *The roots, fruits, lush greenery;*
> *Waterberry, taro, strawberry*
> *Draped and adorned;*
> *As a glamorous bride.*
>
> *Did he show you respect?*
> *When he clad you in a cape;*
> *Did he give you titles?*
> *I think of you today and notice.*
>
> *Nature's trumpet and bugle*
> *The sound of alarm, at your square*

> *Who is there to mind?*
> *And rise to be your shield.*

> *I longed for you in my travels*
> *To reach you, my humble home.*
> *Only to find you in ruins*
> *My yearning changed to gloom.*

I forget the other verses. I am surprised I actually remember all these verses. I wonder if my memory was enhanced when I became a dog? Oh, I recall a few more lines:

> *Brace yourself with your greens*
> *Rise... please rise Yirga Alem*
> *Colour of my childhood dream*
> *The ray that made my eyes open*
> *Over that golden horizon.*

The town's beauty is the lush greenery around her. Just like Babylon, Yirgalem is found between two rivers. Had the rivers been named Euphrates and Tigris, I would have called Yirgalem "Babylon." But Yirgalem is not really Babylon. Yirgalem is like a paradise placed between two rivers; the rivers Woyma and Wamele nurture the lush green pastures of the town. Upstream, going down the mountains, Wamele is also known as Apollo. When the river flows downstream, around the town, it's name changes to Wamele. Woyma also has another name upstream. It is called Abakassa until it reaches town. The two rivers go all around the town from each side, and finally merge into one river called Gidaw. If it snowed in the area between the middle of town to where the two rivers join, it would make a great ski slope. It goes so steeply downhill that I can't walk. I skid and roll down involuntarily, until I reach the bridge.

Between the bridge and the natural hot spring, the road goes all the way uphill. A few cars crawl along slowly. Horse-drawn carts creak away. Looking at the horses dragging their load, I am happy I didn't turn into a horse. Had I turned into a horse in this town, someone would have taken advantage; loading me and flogging me for the rest of my life. One of the horses that is drawing a cart looks battered. When the horse draws the cart forward, the load on the cart pulls him back. The cruel driver flogs the horse with a whip. I wonder if the horse will make it to the top of the hill alive.

'Go!' says the driver, and whips again.

I don't even think he does it deliberately. Maybe his hand is just used to doing it. If this cart driver is reborn in the form of a horse, as with Eastern beliefs, the battered horse is bound to be reborn as a cart driver. He would then realize what it is like to be a horse. I can't stand the sight of the poor horse any longer. I hasten my pace to go past them. I think of the horse as Ethiopia and the cart driver as the political leaders. Thoughtless leaders, prodding the wounded as they herd them along—an evocative metaphor for Ethiopia's current state of affairs.

I am back on my journey again. I just left the town of Yirgalem behind me. I see that the red soil has covered peoples' shoes and clothing, giving everything a red hue. I am now heading towards the city of Hawassa.

I see rows of smoke-wreathed mud huts to my right and left. Most of them have enset plants growing in their backyards. The pointy roofs of the huts among the leafy plants give the impression of a soldier with a drawn sabre. It's also not unusual to see some coffee plants among the leafy enset plants. Commuter buses, loaded with the herb khat, speed past me to reach Hawassa. One of them nearly hits me. Not only the drivers, but also the buses themselves seem high on the stimulant; as though they were fuelled by khat instead of petrol.

On the way from Yirgalem to Hawassa there are several small rural towns; Aposto, Anferara, Moroche, Habella, Tulla and Monopol. I realise that coming from the direction of Hawassa, on the road that goes to Moyale, the town of Yirgalem is a few miles along the side road that goes to Aposto.

All the houses I see on my way from Yirgalem to Hawassa look like bird wings. I find the red paintings on the mud walls entertaining. This particular painting would have made me laugh out loud if I had been a human. The painting shows a hunter killing a wild animal. It is difficult to tell whether the animal is a lion or a leopard. The hunter is kneeling to shoot. Rows of bullets, which actually look like flies, head towards the animal. The short distance between the hunter and the animal gives one the impression that the hunter is actually showing his gun to the animal, rather than shooting it.

The other huts have some election posters still stuck to them. The victory sign used as a logo by the Kinijit party has one finger missing. Next to it there is a poster for a party with a bee logo. The bee in the picture is as big as a bull. The posters remind me of the spectacularly rigged election of 2005. I pass by the house, just as that election ignored so many houses and marched past. If I stop every now and then, like I am doing now, I wonder when I will reach Addis Ababa! I can't resist making another stop at a mead vendor. The sign reads: "Dodge and Taste Mead Wine." Oh dear, I had better get on with my journey and at least make it to Hawassa by nightfall.

Nine

Getting to the palace is not going to be as easy as I thought. Had I not heard of the news of the Prime Minister's ill-health I would have sneaked onto a lorry going to Addis by now, but I was worried about people blaming his ill-health on me. What if they say I have given the Prime Minister rabies? I have purposely avoided close contact with any dogs. I even refrained from chasing the puppy that snatched the goat's head in mid-air for the same reason.

Strangely, I was thinking just the other day about how the Prime Minister would do anything to stay in power. Was it some kind of a premonition? I was worried about him having a similar dream to the Comoros Prime Minister. I was convinced that he was similarly capable of exterminating all the dogs in the country if that happened. Once African leaders get into the saddle of power, they think no one can possibly get them down, even death. When they die, they want the horse they have been riding to die with them.

Keen to hear more about the Prime Minister's sickness, I left my intended path for about an hour and followed a group of people going somewhere else:

'The rumour is—he is severely sick. Some even say it is graver than that. A newspaper that reported he is gone was shut down.'

'What is new about all this? Both sickness and death are unavoidable. The man is not God, so he won't live forever. It is a pity he lost his chance. Had he conceded in the 2005 election, he would always have been honoured as the father of democracy. If he dies now, only his party members will be grieving for him. How did the country benefit while he was in power? Torn apart—ethnic hostilities, discrimination, and corruption? He even denied people their right to speak freely and express themselves.'

'Well said. If he had the guts, why didn't he get treatment in his own country, like the Ghanaian president? A sure sign that the country has not made much progress is the fact that he chose to get treatment abroad. On the contrary, the Ghanaian president was treated and buried with honour in his own country. It's better to get treated and die in your own country than to go abroad and get well. Why does he get better treatment abroad when the rest of his people don't have the same privilege? Shame on them! Do they mean to tell us that not everyone is entitled to get special treatment during sickness, but every citizen is equal in death?'

'The lack of good education and professionalism in the country may have made him lose confidence in the doctors.'

'How about his doubts...? "A dog with a wounded bottom cannot bark out loud," doesn't this saying ring true in his case? Apart from the lack of quality healthcare, who could he possibly trust to put him under sedation? After all, he is responsible for putting together the very same education policy that is incapable of producing good doctors. The senior doctors, who had better education, have left the country in search of a better life.'

Fed up with listening to these endless debates between travellers, I turned back and headed towards Hawassa.

I wish I had wings to get me to Arat Kilo palace, to watch first-hand the dramatic power-grab. Surely this is a historical moment. I wish I could see the Kingmaker masterfully at work, like in the days of Ras

Michael Sihul; I wonder if Sibhat Nega will continue to play his part?

I just remembered—what a coincidence! Before Sibhat Nega became a guerilla fighter, he used to be the director of a reputable school in the town I just left; Yirgalem. At the time, going to this school was considered as good as going to university. The famous author by the same name, Sibhat Gebre Egziabher, though now deceased, also used to teach at the same school.

I start running again. I am nearly there; Hawassa. From there to Addis Ababa is less than three hundred kilometres. The legendary patriot, Bekele Woya, ran on the same road I am running on to Borena, where he fought the invading Italian army. With all the sacrifices so many patriots have made for this country, I don't understand how the country seems to have so little to show for it. Stepping on the same road that Bekele Woya trod makes me feel courageous.

As I get closer to Hawassa, I think about the small towns I pass. Morecho is the junction that goes to Blate, one of Ethiopia's largest military training camps. It has an airstrip for large military transport aircraft.

I remember taking a turn at Leku. Leku, a city slightly off the main highway, used to be a capital during King

Menelik's regime, until Balcha Aba Nefso transferred the capital to his birthplace; Hagere Selam. Then Ras Desta Damtew transferred the capital to Yirgalem. Ras Desta chose Yirgalem because the complicated road structures and bridges that surrounded the city were ideal for defence. Haile Selassie used to imprison his rivals, including Lij Eyasu's relatives, in the same city. Lij Iyasu's relatives were allowed to move within the city, but they were banned from crossing the river.

There are several similarities between Haile Selassie and the present prime minister, Meles Zenawi; their short stature, their cruel nature—Machiavellian, vindictive, patronizing, megalomaniac—a similar God-complex. On these reminiscences, I get to Hawassa.

I will look for some food and water in this city and then carry on my journey. I am eager to be at the palace while the news is still hot. If the prime minister hadn't been responsible for depriving the country of potential leaders, neither his sickness nor his death would be such a big deal. Any potential leaders have either been forced to emigrate or are serving time in prison. In his desire to shine as bright as the sun, he has got rid of all the other sources of light except the very dim ones. Now the battle for power will be among the dim.

Ten

My sharp ears have been picking up news about the prime minister's death like a satellite dish.

'I heard they used radiation to kill him,' says a man with a very shrill voice, turning around to check that there were no spies nearby. 'The Ghanaian president, who was sitting near him at the meeting, and another African leader also had the same fate.'

'Who would do that? Why do we try to change common rumours into proven facts?' says another guy.

'It's not a common rumour. You see, the Westerners are terribly wary of African leaders. So, to get away with their conspiracies in the continent, they need to deal with the clever leaders first. You can see that, when three people sitting in row die one after the other, this is not a coincidence.'

'I really don't understand what you mean by "radiation". Nuclear radiation is not something you control like a handheld torch. If it is used in one conference hall it will kill everybody, not just three black leaders.

I don't think our people understand the difference between nuclear radiation and voodoo.'

'I may not know better than you, but I think he was cursed by Waldiba monks,' says another person.

'How could a monk's curse strike the other guys that were sitting next to him?' asks the guy with a shrill voice.

'That's a good question. You see, when monks in the olden days cursed, their hex used to work for seven generations. These days the monk's curse spreads to the seven people sitting next to the person that was cursed. So, while old curses used to be communicable by birth, now it is by seats.'

'*Ha ha ha...* In that case, the next generation should turn the Waldiba monastery into a military defence camp. While countries like Iran dream of nuclear refineries, we will develop our Waldiba monastery. That way, when powerful nations plan to use nukes on us, we will use our monks' curses first. *Ho ho ho...*'

'Hey Brother, this is not a joke.'

'The cause of the Ghanaian President's death has been made public. His treatment was not kept secret like our Prime Minister's. Like the saying goes: "A deceased calf's neck is long."—there have been efforts to make the Prime Minister look angelic, and his death saintly. I have also heard some say that his cause of death was overwork.'

'Are you saying that he didn't have a heavy workload?'

'We can't say that he didn't—he worked real hard to eliminate any opposition parties, he worked hard to promote differences within the public, he also worked hard to develop ethnic federalism. He put much effort into magnifying his achievements... but these cannot possibly have caused his death. We've never even heard reports of miners, working in dangerous conditions, dying of overwork. Anyways, all he had to do was oversee policies, not actually implement them personally. Meles was a great politician, not a great leader. To say that he died of exhaustion would be the same as insulting ministers and other officials as idlers. We've never even heard of an international politician, responsible for the high stakes global political agenda, dying of overwork. Why do we make ourselves such a laughing stock?'

'How about the speculation that the journalist Abebe Gelaw petrified him to death?' asks a middle-aged man, who has been listening quietly thus far.

'If he indeed died of a panic attack, that would make him the second ruler to die of panic in Ethiopian history. King Iyzor was crowned in Axum in 772^AD. On the day of his coronation, every resident of Axum went out to pay tribute. The whole morning, the drumming, the serenading went on... Iyzor then passed away from a panic attack. The legend is he ruled for only half a day.

'The difference between Iyzor's death and Meles' is that Iyzor died of adulation, while the other died of humiliation. If Meles was petrified by the simple public confrontation that a journalist brought abroad, then it shows how he was not used to any criticism or genuine debate within his own parliament. Towards the end, apart from filling the parliament almost exclusively with his party, the members could ask only pre-arranged questions—given to them. It looked like a theatrical performance; the protagonist had no problems acting. On top of that, Meles must have heard that Napoleon Bonaparte feared "four journalists more than a thousand bayonets" while researching "Bonapartism"—an ideology he frequently referred to in public. Why else was he so terrified of press freedom towards the end? He made sure the few existing newspapers and magazines were shut down, and most journalists were either imprisoned or emigrated before he died.'

'How about the claim that internal strife within the party caused his death?' asks another quiet listener, this one wearing a hat.

'Who on earth would dare to challenge Meles locally? More likely, Westerners might have plotted his death because of his favouritism towards China, who want to gain economic influence in Africa.'

'Stop right there, Champ! Why would you dispute the most logical reason for his death? It is known that he had a brain tumour for a while. You know, he wasn't made of iron. Why would we discount his condition? What I find surprising is why famous Ethiopians mostly die after brain surgery—to mention only a few, there was Engineer Kitaw, Laureate Tsegaye Gebre Medihin, and Meles Zenawi.'

'Oh, what are you implying...?'

'What if Ethiopia drills oil from people's brains... *hee hee hee...*'

The bantering goes on. Everybody, unabashed, makes his guess. I can say, apart from me, everybody had a say. Had I not been a dog, I would have said what I think as well. This reminds me of the adage: "If you are unable to speak for yourself, others will fill in the gap with rumours." If the facts about the prime minister's death had been made public, all these rumours wouldn't have occurred.

In any case, the prime minister's death has made the public awash with crocodile tears and caused an avalanche of rumours. The political cadres, who are known for their tiresome propaganda, add to this mayhem. They say similar things over and over again until one actually loses sight of who said what. The prime minister's death is shocking, no doubt. If I had been a person, I would have considered it natural to feel sorry or cry for the deceased. But, from what I hear, the grieving is exaggerated. Every community seems to be competing to host the most elaborate mourning service.

Everyone seems fed up with the lengthy mourning. "It is not good to grieve too much; it attracts more death." Why the big deal, anyway? Ethiopia has lost so many patriots before. It is truly sad to die at the age of fifty-seven. But these pretensions, to make the death seem graver than it is, are not right. Death obscures the ill-doings of the deceased, but the fact remains he was responsible for the country's lack of future leaders.

This reminds me of a similar anecdote. A man who lost his wife was at the edge of her freshly dug grave. During the funeral, he bowed down to cry for his departed wife, when a 50 birr note fell out of his chest pocket into the grave. The gravediggers, who didn't notice this, covered the grave with soil, along with the money. The man cried even more saying: "Oooh, in her death she dragged me down to the pit!" The Ethiopian public seems to have the same mood; crying not so much for the loss of a leader but for the fact that he has dragged the country down to the pit.

I start listening to the discussions again.

'The prime minister also worked unashamedly at making sure that there were no strong opposition parties. He worked tirelessly at this, as much as he worked on development policies. The country no longer has distinct borders. He has worked hard at accomplishing the task that the Westerners assigned him. He has died of exhaustion...'

As the man continues to jabber, another bloke sharply cuts him short.

'Let the deceased be and focus on those who live,' says the frustrated chap. 'This is the problem with us Ethiopians. We try to make up for our shortcomings by putting the blame on the past, rather than working to improve what's at hand. Let Meles rest in peace, and focus on what's at hand! We should consider our fixation with ripping apart and starting all over again; it is time to learn to repair the damage. We should stop blaming all evils on the past system. Meles got nowhere doing that to Menelik. From now on, we should learn from his mistakes, instead of putting all the blame on him.

'The new leadership must be a better one. Our country has a long history. Many leaders have come and gone. So this is not something new. As the proverb states: "It is better to tell the truth and face the outcome." We have to admit that this is about our nation, not about a particular person. The new leaders have to be very careful. They have to be broad-minded. They should patiently handle the transition.

'The issue of tribal and religious intolerance is getting quite grave. The economy is not doing great either. Apart from this, we have offended volatile Egypt by starting the Nile Dam project. This seems a convenient time for Al-Shabaab attacks. The new leaders should take their wary eyes off their citizens and watch our international opponents.'

I wish I could have added something to that, but sadly I'm a dog. I don't have the ability to speak.

As you know, my original plan was to go to the palace at Arat Kilo. My only worry then was how to get through the palace fence. When I reached Hawassa, I heard more of the prime minister's death. I also overheard many people are going into the palace to pay their respects to the deceased. I am envious. I guess most of them are there to see what the palace looks like. Unlike the old system, there are no longer royal banquets at the palace, so this seems like a good chance to get to see it.

This is also a good chance for me to get into the palace, along with the mourners. But I am too far away. I won't make it. Well, I might as well continue my spying on Hawassa's public.

This is a decisive moment. I should eavesdrop on different sectors of Southern society. I am not threatening to anyone. Nobody would suspect me of spying.

I am surprised to hear someone, who looked grief stricken when he was interviewed on TV the other day, now harshly criticizing the prime minister. These are useful times, I should get as much information as I can.

There is a lesson in seeing a country with three thousand years of history go through the quandary of not having a capable leader to replace a deceased one. We should have been spoiled for choice, from among many suitable candidates. We are not that lucky. But we have to learn a great lesson from this and avoid getting in a similar quagmire in the future. Thus I need to get all the information I can get now, lest we forget this moment in the future.

Eleven

For the last few days, the storm of rumours blowing from one edge of town to the other, made me forget that I was a dog.

The prime minister was buried. The public broke their musical fast. Several nightclubs, which were caught playing music during the mourning period, were closed down. After the funeral, they paid the regular bribe and reopened. Now they blast music from different regions of the country, and urge their clientelle to dance along. From Gondar's neck dance, which reminds one of a busy spy, to Tigray's circular shuffle; the shivers of the Gojam, which bring to mind a malaria patient, to the Oromo's horse-like prancing—all were on display, like evidence of the ethnic politics that the deceased prime minister promoted. Those who have missed drinking beer during the mourning period are busy at it. They hold tumblers so massive, they look like they are about to wash themselves, rather than drink.

Hawassa is awakening from her slumber. The city is getting its vibe back. Prostitutes from the Bermuda neighbourhood are getting back to work. They were unable to work for some time now, as if the prime minister's death had emasculated the men. That has passed now. The men are invading Bermuda once more.

I couldn't leave Hawassa. If I were human, I would be spoiled for entertainment. People's lifestyles are not quite conventional here. The person who eats boiled potatoes from a roadside vendor, and the bloke who drives a luxury car; both seem to have the same level of confidence and self-worth. I noticed people of lower means seem to have greater inner strength. It could be because they don't know who to blame for their misfortune, or they have accepted their fate. Either way, they look content.

Hawassa, is a city filled with an assortment of people from different tribes. Their society does not have a common psychology, so individual beliefs seem more prominent.

From what I can tell, life here is expensive. As a city of entertainment and resorts, there are a variety of restaurants and hotels for visitors who flood the city during weekends. However, low-income earners would struggle to make ends meet here.

I frequent the lake-shore in the mornings. They sell fried fish and fish soup there. People, hawks and dogs all scramble for food there. Hence the area gained its name; Hawk's Valley. The hooded vulture promptly arrives, soaring like an aeroplane, it picks up its prey and leaves. People enjoy their fill of fish dishes, loosening their belts at times to make more room; leaving fish carcasses along the lake-shore. Were there not hooded vultures to efficiently stuff their red pouches with carcasses, the shore would come to resemble a killing field. Dogs, including myself, also take part in the clearing of leftover carcasses.

The comfort of readily available food is one of the reasons I couldn't yet leave this city. I also come to this place in the evenings. I have become addicted to eavesdropping on lovers strolling by the lake-shore. Picking up romantic confessions in broken Amharic has become my hobby. These assignations remind me of my wife. Early memories of our romantic days come to my mind.

I can still hear her unfading voice in my ears. I recall her gaze upon my own. I wonder if she has forgotten me? Could she have got over her grieving and replaced me with another? Could her melodic voice be crooning in someone else's ears? Could my children be cringing from a stepfather's chastising looks? Damn you, the evil one, for tempting me to tamper with magic!

My sad thoughts are interrupted by something I hear from a passer by. My goodness, it is already September the eleventh—Ethiopian New Year! Time seems to have passed like a bullet. I had planned to turn back to a human before the New Year. Oh God!

Fate has conspired against me, and many other Ethiopians, that we would slip into the New Year without any change in our lives. In Ethiopia, mountains bloom every year, not the people. The New Year song also never changes, like the people:

> *Have you seen the flowers?*
> *Lush and blooming;*
> *Have you seen the flowers?*
> *Lush and blooming;*
> *Line up my dear friends,*
> *Lush and blooming;*
> *Till I gather wood to build a house,*
> *Lush and blooming*
> *I don't have a house or even a fence,*
> *Lush and blooming*
> *So I sleep in the open, counting the stars,*
> *Lush and blooming*

I see little girls beating their drums to accompany their soft singing. I just noticed something in the verses to this New Year song for the first time.

> *Line up my friends,*
> *Till I gather wood to build my house*

These verses clearly portray the lives of many Ethiopians. They plan year after year, but they can't achieve anything. The nation is used to counting years at a tortoise's pace. The people, from leader to follower, don't know how to appreciate the value of time. Jesters and their spectators don't believe in the virtue of making dreams come true through hard work and determination. I can't possibly change the nation to 'a land of possibilities' by magic. What's magic ever done for me except change me into a dog? I start following the children, and listen to their sweet melody:

> *After counting the stars,*
> *Lush and blooming*
> *I go to my scolding stepmother's house*
> *Lush and blooming*

Maybe my children are singing the same song right now. They may have to replace the phrase, "scolding stepmother's house," with "scolding stepfather's house." I have to leave Hawassa immediately and go to my home in Addis Ababa. I have to delay my plan to go to the palace. I have to see my children and find out my wife's marital status first. My wife is still young and pretty, who would let her stay single this long?

With these thoughts on my mind, I start running.

Twelve

I start following a commuter bus which is blaring the song: "Who let the dogs out?" from its open windows. Its wheels seem to be moving in slow motion towards Shashemene. I am actually interested in the music, not the creaky old bus.

Who let the dogs out?

I like the barking that accompanies the lead singer. When I hear the word "party" in the song, it reminds me of the ruling political party. I feel like this party, which changed its leadership from a Northerner to a Southerner, requested this song for me. In my heart, I request the same song back to them. I am now leaving Menagesha City, the administrative centre of the Southern region, which the newly elected Prime Minister once presided over. I have heard so much about the new prime minister during my stay in Hawassa. From the first instance I heard about his assignment to the role, I went around visiting places he frequented—from the church he worshipped in, to the house he lived in when he was the Regional President.

I could have reached Shashemene by now, if I hadn't spent so much time in the markets, eavesdropping on what people said about the new Prime Minister. He wasn't spared slander; some of the tribal insinuations are hard to repeat. It was sad to hear how many people are possessed by tribalism. Some were just enjoying the banter, like the one I heard in a local bar:

'Why was he appointed on the eleventh?'

'Do you think it is intentional?'

'Of course, of all days, why was he publicly given power on that day?'

'I think it's just a coincidence.'

'Uh uh, it's not a coincidence. They purposely called an urgent meeting to have the House of Representatives inaugurate him on the eleventh—*hee hee*—from now on, "nine-eleven" will be spoken of as a favoured day.'

Another conversation I heard just before the new Prime Minister was officiated went like this:

Haile Mariam Desalegn was on TV, an elderly man from the Southern region raised his glass to the TV and said: *'hage shongara deiyage e kawterene.'* Then he explained to everyone in the bar that this meant in Wolayta language: 'We wish this charming and graceful person could become our king.'

I think the old man knew the history of the region well. He went on to explain:

'Wolayta, means "to merge together." If anyone desires he can become a Wolayta, even a Chinese man.' Everybody got the joke and laughed. The old man was tipsy, but still quite coherent in his speech. 'Wolayta, like I said, is an assortment of tribes, but the two major tribes are "Mala" and "Dogala." So, you can easily find in Wolayta society Amharic or Tigrayan people. If you don't trust me, read your history books.'

'Oh, who are you trying to assimilate with...?' said another old bloke, with a missing tooth.

'I say it is better to gain knowledge than get drunk, old man, why don't you shut up and let the wise man speak? If you have knowledge, share it; if not, at least let the others share theirs.'

'Please go on, Gash Wolansa,' said a middle-aged man who seemed eager to listen to the rest of the story.

'If "Gap-tooth" over there lets me, I will gladly do so.'

'Go on then, I'm all ears!' said the man with the missing teeth, sarcastically.

'The ruling class came from among the Malas, since King Anse came to power. Later on, power was taken by Kawo Michael of the Tigro Malas. The Amaro Dogalas were mainly priests and healers.

'The Tigray tribes came to Wolayta, when a Tigrayan official called Gaim Seyoum came to the region with his beautiful sister. The King at the time, Leche, fell in love with the sister and married her. Michael became the King's General. He was a heroic warrior. The people then assembled, and said: *"hage shongara deiyage e kaw-terene,"*—We wish this charming and graceful person could become our king." Compared with Michael, King Leche was quite dull, and he soon died of natural causes. The people happily carried Michael into the palace and enthroned him.'

'Oh so now, the order is reversed; when Meles of Tigray died, Hailemariam of Wolaita, will replace him as prime minister?' asked the man with a missing tooth.

'You finally got it, "Gap-tooth!" said the old man who was telling the story, getting up to dance a tribal dance.

'Wait a minute, does that mean Hailemariam is descended from the Tigro Wolayta?'

'I don't have to tell you everything, brother. I gave you a hint, you make your own conclusions. I'm not making this up. I'm just sharing historical knowledge.'

'Right, so the Tigrayan party, TPLF, are now emerging as kingmakers. That's like, an entire political organisation taking over the role of the historical kingmaker, Michael Sihul...' said the middle aged man, stretching his neck like an antenna.

As I recall this banter, the old bus is still blaring the song over and over, on its way to Shashemene.

> *Who let the dogs out?*

The song seems to have a double meaning to me. I can't help but put my own words and give them meaning like a poet:

> *Wait for me y'all my dogs,*
> *the party is on, and I can't see a lot*
> *any canine will do, I am figurin',*
> *that's why they call me faithful*
> *'Cause I'm the man of the land*
> *When they see me they doah-oooo*
> *Who let the dogs out?*
> *Woof! Woof! Woof! Woof!*

I am approaching Shashemene. The old bus has gone and left me without a song.

Thirteen

I enter Shashemene town at around noon, panting from dehydration. My tongue sticks out involuntarily and I am drooling.

No matter how I try, I can't control my dog habits. I shouldn't. My human element foolishly tries to interfere with my canine instincts. Unlike humans, who always try to tame nature to suit them, it is only natural for a dog to cool itself by sticking its tongue out, and by drooling. Dogs are not reserved; they do what is natural to them, as they don't have modesty. Humans, however, weigh even their rebellious desires out of a fear of consequences.

I think I have discarded some of these fears since I became a dog. Of course that does not include my fear of getting rabies. I am still terrified of contracting the virus. I pray that God would spare me, and help me get to Addis Ababa while I'm still in good health.

I am heading down the main concrete road towards the Abosto neighbourhood. I just realized that Shashemene's chaos is not ideal for a man or a dog. As it is a commercial town, people bustle around, some carrying their purchases, others slinging them in a bag. It is like a smaller version of Addis Ababa's Mercato; the largest market in Africa. Oh, that reminds me of Laureate Tsegaye Gebremedhin's poem, *Oh Mercato*:

> *...Oh Mercato,*
> *Where folks come from everywhere,*
> *In multitudes to pay you homage,*
> *Laden with stuff and bric-a-brac*
> *Brimming admirers and patrons alike*
> *Exhausted by your breadth and magnitude*
> *Their load made heavier by your offer*
> *Looking wilted, from enterprise and trudge*
> *...Oh Mercato...*

I forget the rest of the poem. Laureate Tsegaye's poems are unforgettable, but maybe it is my transformation into a dog that made me forget it.

The bells from Shashemene's horse-drawn carts remind one of prayer time. Even donkey-drawn carts are supposed to have reflective plate numbers to avoid night-time accidents.

My eyes seem to be attracted to unusual scenes, which I would not have paid attention to as a human.

The auto rickshaw drivers are reckless. They don't give any indication when they pull over or resume their journey. I have nearly been hit about four times. I don't want to die before I see my wife and children.

When I get closer to Abosto neighbourhood, I see a butcher's shop. I go straight to it, like a customer. Irritated by my gawking, the butcher throws a bone at me, which catches me right on my muzzle. Butchers, so far, have been hope-busters for me. They are so mean. I turn back to check if there is any meat on the bone. It is as white as the Himalayan Mountain peaks. There isn't enough on it to feed an ant. How on earth did he manage to take *all* the meat off? I give up on this shop and start looking for another one.

A particular song from a music shop window catches my attention. The song isn't about meat, but from a tribe whose staple food is meat—the Gedeo tribe. I have heard the Gedeo saying—"nothing about a bull is inedible, except the sound it makes." Well, I will have to find something to eat to get my strength up, and get me to Addis Ababa. When I was in Hawassa, I heard two people talk about a new butcher's called "A Hero Won't Die" at Arat Kilo, I hope they will be more generous there. The men were bantering about the Prime Minister's death.

'This pretentious mourning is so blatant that it is sickening.'

'What do you mean?'

'At Arat Kilo...'

'What?'

'They opened a butcher's shop called "A Hero Won't Die" in his memory.'

'Let them commemorate anything they want in his name, why do you care?'

'Such brown-nosing gets on my nerves.'

'Oh, shut up.'

'They used to say he was a good reader, right?'

'Yes?'

'So, instead of talking about his collection of books, why don't they take them out of the palace and open a library in his name?'

'Why?'

'The country is deprived of libraries, not butchers.'

I didn't hear the rest of the conversation. My dog-ears seem to pick out the word "meat" from every conversation. I have developed such a passion for meat. I am sure I will prioritize eating meat over having sex when I return to humanity.

I will go to a butcher and say "hey, butcher!"

"Yes sir," he will reply, instead of throwing a bone at me.

"Give me ten kilos of meat," I will say, and watch him cut piece after piece of meat.

I hope I will get to see that day.

I am covering the entire Abosto neighbourhood, in search of food. Once I have found a solution to my hunger, I will be foraging for news.

Fourteen

I was forced by an injury to stay in Shashemene for the last two weeks. If it hadn't been for this cursed injury to my hind leg, I would have got to Addis Ababa by now. I have been unable to even scavenge for food. For survival, I have been eating things that a man-turned-dog would find revolting in normal circumstances.

It was a butcher who hit me on the left hind leg with a chunky bone. I now hobble on three legs. The way I walk, I won't make it to the nearest town, let alone Addis Ababa. Nevertheless, once I have recuperated a bit, I will continue my journey. In my lifetime, I have come across many challenges that delayed me from reaching my goal, but none of them stopped me from getting there altogether. Even as a dog, I don't want to succumb to any challenge. Such is life—a game of dodging. When we dodge one challenge, hurled at us, another eventually catches us unaware.

I hobble out of Abosto—the centre of the town. I cross the bridge and head north. After a while, I realize I have arrived at the neighbourhood called Melka Oda.

When I hear a few people talking a strange sounding English, I realize I have arrived at the Rastafarian settlement. I have heard that Caribbean people purposely created such strange sounding English during the times of slavery, to avoid being understood by the slave-owners. If that is indeed the case, I wonder why they still choose to speak this way? I realize that, although this mixed language, called *Patois*, has an English base, it requires a lot of tongue twisting and lip manipulation that make the words sound altogether different.

I overhear two people gossiping about a group of Rastafarians they are walking behind.

'This lot are such a bad influence on our youth. They entice them onto a path from inhibition to addiction.'

'But you have to admit, they are devoted to our nation.'

'So much for devotion—they've turned farmers' plots into marijuana plantations. The farmers get more profit from marijuana than what they get for corn. So they've become adherents to this drug," argues the first speaker. He seems to dislike the Rastafarians.

'They are responsible for so many addictions among the youth. The fools smoke this stuff and drowse around like bees whose hive has been smoked. At least smoked hives yield honey, I haven't seen a single good thing out of this lot.'

'*Hee hee hee...* oh, you make me laugh.'

'I'm serious. They are useless.'

'Talking about bees reminds me...' says the second one, wishing to change the subject.

'Oh no... no... don't even go there! I didn't mean the logo of the ruling party. I just meant the natural bee.'

'What do you mean?' the second speaker insists. 'Talking about the party, or bees? I mean, why did you keep so quiet about the new prime minister!' he hints.

'Oh, no. Let's forget about that.'

'What do you mean?'

'They say that he isn't much to talk about.'

'I don't understand...'

'Some say, he is neither suited for deep critique nor admiration. I am afraid they may be right. I can't even say if he has any deep political knowledge. I recently watched him talk on TV, in one of the parliamentary meetings. I was confused to see how aggressive he was. I guess he has learned a lesson or two from the previous PM. He has taken over a parliament with absolutely no opposition party, so why the annoyance? I had hoped things would be different this time.'

'Hoped for what?'

'As this prime minister had not been a guerrilla fighter, like many of the others in the ruling party, I had hoped he would not be as aggressive. Although I didn't expect he would bring about a genuine change, at least I hoped he would be less about lip-service and more about actual development. I had also hoped that he would please the public by releasing political prisoners. It is easy to see that the Ethiopian public is depressed. They need an inspiring leader. Just repeating, "we will carry on," is useless. Who is stopping them? But they should know that the public is fed up with their propaganda. It's like the proverb, "a fool doesn't know when to stop crying." Instead of wearing us out with the same propaganda, day in day out, why don't they work hard and impress us with real results?'

I didn't hear the rest of what they said. I stopped following them. What I gathered from their conversation is that the new prime minister has challenging times ahead of him. The only option he has is to tighten his belt and work real hard.

I shouldn't waste my time like this. I try not to listen to this kind of conversation, but habits are hard to break. I should have been in Addis Ababa by now, and seen my beloved wife. I wonder once again about the marital status of my wife. Could she have married another man? Men would not let such a beautiful princess stay single for long. I wish I could have wings to soar over and get to Addis Ababa right now.

With an effort, I manage to leave Shahsemene behind. The town was founded in 1895, but its chaotic nature seems to defy age well. The billboard ahead says Shashemene suburb is 250 kilometres away from Addis Ababa. A tedious journey awaits me.

As I approach a parked lorry next to a pile of sand, an idea comes to mind. The lorry is loaded with a variety of vegetables, including khat. I somehow clamber up to the top of the sand pile, and strenuously jump over to the back of the open lorry. The pain from my injured leg is excruciating. I try to tolerate the pain and look around where I have landed. On my left is a pumpkin as big as a football and on my right, there is a bundle of khat that looks like a mummified dwarf. The wellington boots in the corner smell like a burst septic tank. Now my worry is about where the lorry's destination might be. It must be Addis Ababa. I have to try my luck.

Fifteen

It has been a horrible few days. I feel like some of the life has been drained from my short dog existence. If I hadn't managed to drag myself into the middle of a corn farm, I would have been taken apart by the merciless scavenging birds by now. Hiding on this farm, I was forced to become a vegetarian—eating corn cobs for survival.

It is because of an auto rickshaw accident that I find myself in these circumstances. If the God of dogs and all creation hadn't spared me, I would have lost my dog life. The rickshaw didn't hit me full on; it hit me on my left buttock, bending me like rubber and tossing me into a ditch. An unseasonal rain had been pouring down all evening. The flood could have carried an elephant, let alone a battered dog. It hauled me along with the garbage of Shashemene—banging me around with any objects it carried along, the flood finally threw me into a small river. The river in its turn dragged me through shrubs, sometimes knocking me against rocks until it deposited me near a cornfield.

That night, I looked like a chick covered in mud. I couldn't get up in the morning, so I spent the whole day baking in the sun. In the evening I summoned all my strength and dragged myself to this cornfield, where I collapsed.

I have no idea how many days I spent in this cornfield. I no longer count the days; just grateful to have survived one day and moved on to the next. It wasn't just an unseasonal rain that caught me off guard; it was also an unseasonal situation. Sadly, this is not only my fate but also the nation's—living day to day. I imagined the nation being robbed of her harvest by unseasonal rain; an unseasonal ideology forcing a crown of thorns on her head; being ruled by an unseasonal leader. Hasn't this nation stood amongst the greatest on earth?—now it is less than the least. Like me, Her people have been dehumanized and joined the realm of dogs; carried along by the whim of the flood. As a twig once fallen into a torrent has no direction of its own, so are the people of this nation. However, we are not to give up.

I shuffle back to the centre of town. I follow the road to Addis Ababa once again, cringing every time I see an auto-rickshaw.

The lorry parked by the sand pile is still there. If it had not broken down, I would have reached Addis Ababa by now. I still don't know what is wrong with the lorry. I waited for it to move for a long time, that day, then gave up and left. If it had moved, the rickshaw wouldn't have hit me. It's no use thinking about the past now.

There is another lorry parked behind the broken lorry. The gap in the blue plastic covering reveals that it is loaded with potatoes. It is not difficult to guess that this one is going to Addis Ababa. I decide to try my luck again. How do I get on board? There is no pile of sand next to this one. I try, until evening, to devise a plan. I try to climb up using my claws, but fail. The only other option is to get on the broken lorry in front, and jump from there to this one. I once again clamber onto the pile of sand and jump to the broken lorry. From there, I try to gauge the distance between the two lorries. If my back was not hurt I could easily do it. Now I am only a sorrier version of the dog that traversed the forest with the grace of a cheetah.

Come what may, I have to jump. If I end up falling onto the concrete road it will be yet more bad luck, but I'm not afraid of taking the chance. My bravado may end up being the death of me. Let God's will be.

One spirit urges me to 'jump', prompting me to take the leap, while another cautious spirit counsels me to 'hold back, or you may never see your wife and children again.' The spirits of "courage" and "fear" thus pull me one way, then the other, until I close my eyes and choose one over the other.

Ever since I became a dog, I have never made such a noise, and I don't think I can ever replicate it. If the musical instruments of the world resonated together, I doubt if they would manage to produce such a noise. It will never be found among the works of Mozart, nor Beethoven, nor Yared. I make this subconscious noise as I jump over to the next lorry. Lord of Creation! I pass out for a few seconds.

I feel like my back has snapped in two. Every bone in my body seems to have shattered. Have I left this world, or am I still among the living? I struggle to open my eyes. I have landed on the potato-laden lorry. I close my eyes again. I don't want to think about what comes after survival. I thought my bones had scattered on the concrete road. After a little rest, I go under the plastic sheeting and burrow myself into the earthy smelling potatoes.

I wonder where the driver is? He is probably at a khat den. For some time, exhaustion and pain take hold of my entire being. Then I hear the lorry's engine start, roaring for a while as the driver presses the gas pedal. Finally, the lorry drifts away from the town, which still bears the spirit of Emperor Haile Selassie within its Rastafarian settlers.

Although I have finally left Shashemene behind, the thought of Haile Selassie still preoccupies my mind. Then I feel like the spirit of Marcus Garvey is shining upon me, just as bright as the full moon on the horizon. If he could only see the current state of Africa, compared to what he had hoped for! If only he knew that today it is a place where people have been dehumanized and have fallen into the ashes—what would he say? If he saw what had happened to Ethiopia, a nation that was once a symbol of independence and the pride of fellow black people, what would he say?

I can hear the animated voices of the driver and his co-driver. I suspect they are high on khat, and maybe also drinking beer. I hear one of them singing Tilahun Gessesse's song, "Your Pose Is Striking."

The lorry suddenly slows down for a lady, thumbing a lift.

'Let's give her a lift. She's a gift from God,' says one of them.

'You're right, the road is dreary without the charm of a woman,' answers the other one.

'Shall we let her in here at the front or at the back?'

'No, let her get on the back. It won't be convenient here. If you get lucky, I'll do the driving.' This one must be the co-driver.

'Yes please! She is a stunner,' says the driver, and he pulls over next to her.

'Where are you off to? Can we help you?'

'I am going to Ziway.'

'No problem, but I'm afraid the front is full,' the driver says quickly.

'Oh, that is fine. I will get on the back.'

The co-driver helps her get on the back of the lorry. On top of worrying if the lorry will go all the way to Addis Ababa, I now start getting anxious about what they intend to do to the woman.

Sixteen

The cold wind blowing from the adjacent lakes of Abaya and Shola seems to be cooling everything, including the clear moon. We pass the towns of Kuyera and Arsi-Negle in the blink of an eye. The woman seems more worried about the speed of the lorry than being with two strange men at night. I also worry about the speed but the scenery of the surrounding area, accentuated by the moonlight, somehow distracts me. Now and then this stunning vista seems to grab the woman's attention as well.

It is beautiful—very beautiful. I can see flickering firelight inside some of the rural huts. The swishing of the dry corn plantation makes a soothing melody as it sways in the blowing wind. The full moon hanging over the eastern horizon lights the sky-scraping mountain ridges; Abyssinian mountain ranges left bare like its people. These mountains testify to Ethiopia's uncontested beauty when looked on from the outside, yet Her interior demands a priest's absolution.

Apart from earning the country its nickname, "the roof of Africa," it is no surprise this landscape has inspired poets and is the envy of strangers. This nation is dubbed "the African Tibet" after the variety of the terrain; from the heights of Mount Ras Dashen, to the volcanoes of Dallol, these peaks have earned the admiration of friends and foe alike. It isn't surprising poets, as well as ordinary people, admire the beauty of the landscapes, but the fact that a dog cannot take its eyes off it is testimony to an unexaggerated marvel.

The people of this country may not be fortunate enough to benefit from the resources found underground, but that doesn't stop them from enjoying the beauty above. I picture the nation's ancient trade of musk, spices and frankincense; with Meroe, the Middle East, and India.

'How about now?' I ask myself. 'Do I see honour and respect floating over the mountains?' No, I don't see it. Why? Because the country is left bare. Apart from the outside beauty, there are no resources to boast about. I take my eyes off the mountain range and look at the woman on the lorry.

Has she seen me yet? To make it easy for her to spot me I move the plastic sheet that partially covers me and sit on my hind legs. I see that she is beautiful. I wonder if she sees a menacing dog in me? She is scared. She is nervously fidgeting in her seat. I get pleasure out of seeing a beautiful woman get nervous. I don't want her to be too scared, though. What if she chose to jump from the moving lorry? Well, I don't know how courageous this woman can be. One's life is determined by one's choices.

The ability to make a decision, in order to achieve one's goal, is basic but not everybody is gifted with the ability to make a balanced decision. On the other hand, not only people but also animals can make instinctive judgments.

A human being's animal nature can prompt them to make instinctive decisions. People can ride on their animal instincts when they love, fight, take fright or reach sexual climax. I can't tell which decision this woman is about to make; a balanced one or an instinctive one.

Before she can make any decisions, I show her that I am not a menacing dog. I curl back on my spot and pull the plastic sheet with my paw to partially conceal myself. I still peer through the opening. She calms down her fidgeting. I think she knows that I am not dangerous. She should. But then, had she screamed she would have been more of a threat to me than I was to her.

It is easy to guess what will happen if she shouts out in fright. The driver will hear her scream and come to check out what is happening. Then he will break my back with all his might, and throw me out of the Isuzu lorry. I would then be left dying in this wilderness. It has been a while since I last considered that my hope of getting to Addis Ababa is thinner than a thread.

We are approaching Langano. I see a long neck moving rhythmically between the acacia trees, which seems to be sporting a well-coiffured afros. It looks like a stick-figure. The shadows cast in the moonlight make the figure seem like a walking stick striding between the trees—but now I see it is actually an ostrich. My attention switches to the number of roadside graves.

These rows of roadside graves used to fascinate me when I was human. The memorial stones show that some of the deceased were Christian while the others were Muslim. Some are engraved with the cross and others have the crescent moon. A few of them have portraits painted on them; portraits done by an unskilled artist. A well-respected local artist probably painted these, so it is inappropriate of me to belittle such work. I see a portrait of a man riding a horse, which looks more like a cow. I feel pity for the relatives who look on this image whenever they remember their beloved. When I think of the possible philosophy behind these roadside graves, it occurs to me that there might be another philosophy buried along with the dead.

While I contemplate, my eyes are caught by a sight; a caravan of camels. It seems to me that Langano's acacia trees were purposely created for the camels. They are just the right height for the camels to nibble on their green foliage. The lorry's speed makes it difficult for me to reflect much on these spectacles. How did we get to Bulbula so fast? Before I know it, we go past Bulbula town; past the bridge that looks like a sculpture.

A few miles on, I see a bunch of aloe vera, kleinia and cactus growing at the side of the road. I feel sorry for the kleinia, as the prickly cactus growing next to it looks like Diablo's palms about to strike it. 'Are these plants possibly related?' I ponder. Aloe vera, kleinia and cactus. The poor kleinia is sandwiched between the two unpleasant plants. The thorns of the cactus, and the bitterness of the aloe are its eternal fate. My fate, to be a dog, also seems to coincide with the fate of this land.

I shake myself out of this reverie and look at the woman. I can't believe my eyes—the driver is sitting next to her. He talks to her softly. The loud engine noise makes it difficult to hear what he is saying. It is not difficult to guess what is going on, though. She shuffles away from him in her seat, he shuffles nearer.

The co-driver is driving at a higher speed than the driver did. The shuffling game between the driver and the woman goes on a little while longer. When it starts to look like she can't shake him off, she slaps him on the face. He doesn't seem to mind the slap much. She stands up. The wind lifts her dress up. The driver also gets up. She screams. The vast empty space swallows up her cry for help. Again, I think she might be considering jumping off the truck. I imagine her body crashing onto the concrete road. But the driver doesn't let that happen. He topples her onto the seat and gets on top of her.

I have a strong urge to jump on him. I want to sink my teeth into his flesh. If I do decide to obey this urge, I have no doubt I will end up being the victim. My hopes to ride all the way to Addis Ababa on this lorry will be dashed. I will end up in this deserted land. But this woman has absolutely no hope of getting away from this driver unharmed unless I do something. So whatever fate holds for me, I decide to rescue the woman.

As everyone is a victim of his or her decisions, so is every dog. I jump out of my hiding place and bite his leg. He screams.

Were we not approaching Ziway city, this decision would not only have endangered me, but also the woman. The driver's mate brakes so quickly, he almost loses control. In the same instant, I see the woman jump out. As the lorry halts by the side of the road, she manages to avoid the concrete and lands on the dirt deposited by the recent flood.

I have caused serious injury to the driver. For the first time, I taste blood. As he moans and wriggles with pain, I follow the woman and jump from the lorry. I land on the same dirt, but the woman has already run about twenty metres away. I grab her abandoned purse with my teeth and run after her into the woods.

She runs for a couple of minutes and pauses to listen for any pursuing footfalls. Apart from distant hyena howls, neither the driver nor his mate can be heard following. She quietly dives down onto the ground. I can imagine her heart beating fast against the hard ground. I drop her purse in front of her and crouch down beside her. She looks at her purse with disbelief, and then at me. I gaze back at her, my eyes twinkling in the moonlight.

I wonder what she thinks of my eyes. Does she find them scary? Nevertheless, I am her only trusted companion at this moment. The way I see it, I'm almost an angel. Fighting her fear she forces her fingers to my head to show her gratitude. Her fingers shake individually, as if she is practising a string instrument. She hesitantly lays them on my head. I slowly close my eyes in acknowledgment. When I open my eyes, I see her smiling. I wish I could smile back in return... then worry takes over. What will become of us now?

Seventeen

The dangers I anticipate never come to pass. After a while, we hear the Isuzu ram its engines and leave. We make sure it has left, then resume our journey. We still hear the yowl of the hyenas from afar but none come nearer. It seems to me that the hyenas of the rift valley hound only with their cries, not with their teeth. It is evident from her purposeful walk that even the woman is not afraid of the hyenas. We dogs are good at sniffing out fear. I don't smell any fear coming from this woman, instead she seems preoccupied by something else.

She may be thinking about the attempted rape. I hear her say 'scumbags!' aloud, between her thoughts. As I walk behind her, the term rings in my ears. I don't think she is referring only to the driver. Although I am gifted at sussing out fear, I cannot read minds. So, I can't figure out what she is thinking about exactly. My guess is that she is referring generally, to the generation of scumbags produced by the nation's ever-degraded morality . This generation's critics call them "scumbags," "cockups," ... "depraved," "irresolute," and so on. But nobody investigates what actually caused a moral failure of this proportion, or what the solution might be. It is also appropriate to ask: What did the present generation inherit from the past? Did they inherit ruthlessness, betrayal, selfishness, and greed? How about duplicity and brown-nosing? Did the previous generation's Judases teach their children to mend their pockets and carry on in their footsteps? What would be the answer to these questions?

Does despising this generation achieve any good? Failing to ask, "what have I contributed to the next generation?" is like trying to reap what is not sown in the first place: *"No one puts new wine into old wineskins. For the wine would burst the wineskins, and the wine and the skins would both be lost. New wine calls for new wineskins."*

As the wise proverb demonstrates, it is dangerous to try and force the new generation to fit into the perceptions of the old generation. Both the wine and the wineskin need to be checked.

The previous generation's relics need to be tested before being bequeathed to the next generation. Instead of despising this generation for what it has become, the guardians should have been more discerning about what they nourished it with. Having said this, it does not mean that the critics' assertions about this generation are wrong; they are quite apparent.

This beautiful woman walking ahead of me has obviously faced this danger first-hand. If it hadn't been for my sharp teeth, she would have been raped. What is to blame for degenerating the youth? Rampant substance abuse, the sex and pornography industries.

In my previous life, I remember reading papers reporting that one of the gravest problems facing Ethiopians today is alcohol abuse. The reason for such high rates of alcoholism is the hopelessness caused by socio-economic discontent.

Engrossed in these thoughts, I become unaware of how long we have travelled, until we arrive at Ziway. The whiff of spicy stew lingering in the city tells us that we have arrived after dinnertime. My sharp nose can pick up more than smells from cooking pots left ajar; it can even prospect for oil tunnels underground.

Once we reach the city, I think about leaving the woman and heading my own way, but my loyal dog nature prompts me to escort her home. I don't know how much longer this special loyalty, which I presume is linked to my being a dog, will disrupt my journey. She leaves the main road and turns left to Basha neighbourhood, behind the tourist hotel. This area is nicknamed "brawlers' neighbourhood." One can even lie about being from this area, to strike fear. As we come to the end of a gravel road she knocks at a silver gate.

The slender woman that opens the gate immediately starts pouring out torrents of admonishments.

'You! Is there a reason for staying out this long, or is this some kind of rebellion?' she asks shifting her gaze between her and me.

'Imama, I had to submit a long report to my manager, so I had to leave work late... on top of that, I couldn't find any public transport. If you saw the piles of paperwork we had to deal with, you wouldn't believe our actual work is healing people. I told you before, my manager orders me around like he owns me...'

From her reply I have gathered that the woman who opened the gate is her mother, that she is a health professional, and her manager is bothersome.

'What on earth have you dragged along with you?'

This question makes me snap out of my thoughts about the manager. The woman lets her daughter in and quickly slams the gate on me. I should have known that I could only escort the woman to her gate.

Nevertheless, the slammed gate makes me homesick and melancholic. I can verify that a dog's melancholy is graver than a person's. Dogs can't cry. Tears can be therapeutic and wash away grievances. Being unable to cry has created a big pile of wrongs that I keep burying. What a pile of dynamite. Nothing can ever set this dynamite to explode except tears. This brings Be'alu Girma's short poem to mind:

> *Alas I feel like crying,*
> *A lump in my throat*
> *But tears, where've they gone*
> *The ducts have all dried.*
>
> *I feel like laughing*
> *But my teeth only smirk*
> *Crying whilst I laugh*
> *The fate of my poor soul.*

Having become a dog, I can confirm that laughing and crying are a human being's greatest gifts.

I can hear the two women arguing about whether to let me in or not.

'What if it is a rabid dog?' the mother asks. Her voice is not as thin as one would expect from a person with such a scrawny figure, rather it rumbles along like the deepest bass of the blues. The contrast between her skinny figure and her deep voice indicates a nasty character. If I were a psychologist, I would be able to tell why the woman ended up being so cruel by analysing the relationship between her slight stature, ugly looks and deep voice. Researchers should study the relationship between ugliness and spitefulness.

On the other hand, the daughter's beauty makes one wonder if the woman is just her stepmother. I wonder how some unattractive people end up having beautiful children? I know I am harsh; picking on this woman because she shut the gate on me.

The daughter opens the gate wide and, pointing at me, she starts to explain how I cannot be a rabid dog. It is easier to explain health than sickness.

'How could he be rabid? It's not possible. You know why? Rabid dogs lose muscle control and droop their tail between their legs. Have you seen this dog's tail? Look how it stands erect above his back.'

When I hear this, I unconsciously turn around to see my tail. She is not lying.

'Wait... since when did you start loving dogs?'

'Imama—if only you knew what he has done for me? He rescued me like a guardian angel. I think I will name him Angel.'

'Wow, how fitting! They say angels help in picking out names!' says the mother sarcastically.

'Imama, trust me. I assure you this dog is healthy. If you still worry though, I promise I will take him in the morning and get him vaccinated.'

When I hear this, my heart jolts with joy. I don't want to give them time to keep arguing. I dash between their legs into the compound. The daughter closes the gate and locks it. The mother is left speechless.

Eighteen

I have been waiting for weeks to get the promised vaccination. I gather that the daughter is named Atete. I don't know why they gave her that name, but I like it.

While I wait, I venture further than Basha neighbourhood and wander around the whole of Ziway city. Otherwise, the days would become very dreary.

Ziway city, a hundred and sixty kilometres from Addis Ababa, has recently acquired a new name: Batu.

Ancient Oromo tribesmen, who travelled from Bale to Hara searching for pasture for their flocks, came up with the word "Batu." They uttered "Batu" when they laid their eyes for the first time on this oasis by the lake. It means, "God granted us a land that we desired." The word can also mean "you are able," or "you can bear."

On the other hand, Ziway—the old name—has a different meaning altogether. In my previous life, an elderly man explained to me that the word was derived from the Ge'ez phrase "Zi Waiy." This refers to the place's hot and humid nature, being located within the rift valley. Priests from the Kingdom of Axum named the place Ziway when they arrived, fleeing from the plunder and destruction of notorious Queen Yodit. They saw that this humid lakeside town was a good place to hide the Ark of the Covenant.

Most Ethiopian cities have had their names changed. In recent years Awassa was changed to Hawassa, Alaba to Halaba, Alemaya to Haromaya, Nazareth to Adama, Debre Zeit to Bishoftu.

The reason for these changes was to condemn the previous feudal administration, and replace the dominant culture with the indigenous one. It is a symbolic gesture.

The lakeside city of Ziway currently has over fifty thousand residents. I don't believe there is a census of the dog population in this city. What I do know is that the abattoir is located in the suburbs, which is not suitable for dogs; a city is not a city if there are no abattoirs within the city centre. A city can only be deemed a "city" if its dog population can eat well and bark as they should. Nobody should expect a single bark from the dogs in this humid city, panting instead with their protruded tongues, preoccupied with sustenance. If the lake was not here, this city would not be a desirable place to dwell. The cool breeze from the lake gives a welcome relief.

There is a legend that tells of the formation of Lake Ziway. In the olden days the lake used to be a well. People were expected to cover it with a lid when they finished drawing water. One day, a mother went to the well with her clay pot to draw water. Hearing her child cry from afar, she hurried back without covering the well. The water started flooding the meadows, creating islands. The people who escaped the flooding started to live on the islands.

Although this is not a credible account, the lake indeed has five islands. They are called Gelila, Debre Sina, Debre Zion (Tulu Gudu), Gethsemane (Findro), and Abraham (Tsedecha). There are churches on all the islands.

Several religious relics, including replicas of the Ark of the Covenant, were spared from destruction, as they were hidden in these churches in times of war. Later on, new churches were planted in other parts of the country and these surviving relics were moved there. It is recorded that the Ark of Saint Gabriel, hand crafted by Saint Mark the Apostle, was taken from an island in Ziway and placed in Kulubi Gabriel Church in Dire

Dawa. To this day, people who hunt for the Ark of the Covenant have not taken their eyes off the islands of Ziway. This reminds me of an anecdote by the British author, Graham Hancock.

In his search for the Ark, Hancock went to Debre Zion Island in Ziway. He started firing questions at the welcoming monk:

'Do you believe that the Ark of Zion was brought to this island?'

'Absolutely,' replied the monk, without hesitation.

'Why was it brought here?'

'To spare it from destruction by Queen Yodit.'

'How long was it kept here?'

'For seventy two years.'

'Where was it taken after that?'

'To Axum.'

'Was it ever brought back after that?'

'Never.'

'I heard that there is a book that explains how the Ark of Moses was brought here. Is this true?'

'Yes!' The monk's expression changing as he replied.

'Can I see it?'

'You can... but the part about the Ark has been ripped out. A man came here about twenty years ago; he ripped out and took all the pages that related the story of the Ark.'

'Was it a foreigner?'

'No, it was an Ethiopian. Searching for this man is futile.'

Thus, Hancock's search for the Ark got even more complicated.

If I were an author I would have used "The Ripped Pages" as the title for a book. I think of this as I sit by the Ziway lakeshore and look across at the islands.

About fifteen thousand people from the Zai tribe live on the islands. If one were to call Zai a melting pot of Ethiopian tribes, it wouldn't be a lie. The Zai are composed of Tigray, Amhara, Oromo, Gurage—several tribes' blood surging as one. The variety of dialects among the Zai testifies to this. These are people who live consistently in faith, whether in times of flight or times of joy. History records that the Zai people were highly tested during the time of the great famine. In those dreadful days, while people searched for grains in cattle droppings in other parts of Ethiopia, the Zai people survived by boiling animal hide for food. Those who were too weak to fish were known to exchange land for fish guts. One can also recall from their history times of joy and happiness.

I have been to these islands I am now gazing at, when I was a man deeply involved in the occult. I made deep enquiries about their wizard, Atqu.

Atqu went to these islands to defend the religious relics during the raid of Amhad ibn Ibrahim, also known as Ahmad Gragn. He and the people who followed him formed a clan known as Wiyzero. One of the things that made this clan stand out was their observance of Kosher laws. The reason being, they believed they were Jews, and in remembrance of Jacob's battle with the angel and how the angel struck Jacob's thigh, they did not eat meat from the passage of an animal's sciatic nerve.

The wise wizard Atqu wanted to challenge Amin Ab, the island's reigning leader, for his position. This contest required him to solve a riddle.

The riddle was: Which weighs more? A grain of barley or a sheaf of barley?

'A grain of barley!' said Atqu quickly.

'How can a grain weigh more than a whole sheaf? The sheaf weighs more!' said Amin Ab.

'The grain!'

'The sheaf!'

'Let them be weighed.'

'Let them be weighed.'

A weighing scale was brought. A grain of barley was put on one side and a sheaf of barley on the other. The grain weighed more. They tried it again. Again, the grain weighed more. Atqu won.

As agreed, Atqu became the new ruler. However, as a grain of barley could never weigh more than a sheaf of barley, everyone knew that he had won the contest by using magic. When I was a human, I went to great lengths to acquire Atqu's notes on magic. I documented several of his legends.

I finally take my eyes off the islands and focus on myself and my current situation. I must go back to Basha neighbourhood, to Atete's house. I don't know why she has become nonchalant about my vaccination. How can I possibly remind her? I can only make the sounds of a dog. I look like a dog. I wonder if I can ever turn back to a human being? I don't know.

Nineteen

This morning, two ideas passed back and forth in my mind like shuttles on a weaver's loom: do I wait for vaccination? Or carry on with my journey? I have decided that whatever happens has to happen today.

I wait for Atete to wake up and open her bedroom door. Then I try to act like a rabies-infected dog. I let my tail fall limp between my legs. The very next minute, it occurs to me what I'm doing is actually wrong. An infected dog would probably be put down, not vaccinated. As soon as I realize this, I spring my tail back upright. Too late; Atete has already noticed. She stares at me for a moment with a worried frown and goes back to her room. I start to squirm with anxiety.

I wonder if she remembers her mother's cautious remark: 'What if it is infected?'

'She will probably give me poisoned meat for my next meal,' I think. I should flee right now—if only somebody would open the gate.

I also imagine the neighbours stoning me to death. I can see their cruel faces in my mind's eye, and I hear their shouts of excitement in my head. Suddenly, Atete yanks the door open and steps out. I can't move—fear pins me to the spot. She immediately slips the metal chain on my neck and starts dragging me to the gate. I have no other alternative but to follow her. I wonder if she is leading me to immunization or execution.

My gut feeling tells me Atete is not going to have me put down.

I am not wrong. After several minutes, my long-awaited vaccination is done. I will no longer cringe away from neighbouring dogs in fear.

This implies that I have a better chance of living the full average life expectancy of a dog. If I am denied living a human life, then it is not an easy feat to accept that I am a dog and must live as one. Leading one's life in constant comparison with others is a curse. I am no longer going to lament my short lifespan.

The animal with the shortest lifespan I know of is the Golden-ringed May Dragonfly. It lives in wet surroundings for a single day. But it fulfils its purpose in life within this short time. It finds a mate and, with its gilt wings, dances with her and procreates. Whether it eats plenty and enjoys glorious weather, or eats little and has miserable weather, it still fulfils its intentions before expiring at the end of the day.

I wonder what I would have done if the magic had turned me into this insect? I think a day wouldn't have been long enough to think about what I would do, let alone fulfil it. Yet, this insect has spare time for relaxation. It is often seen leisurely floating on lake-shores.

Even bees, renowned for their hard work, can only live for twenty-eight days—just enough time to make honey. A bee's existence may seem brief from my perspective, but for them it is nothing short of a regular lifetime.

In contrast, clams found in the North Atlantic, known as Ocean Quahog, are renowned for their longevity. These clams not only keep safe within their shell but also bury themselves in sands at the bottom of the sea.

I believe it is better to fly freely for a single day, like the May dragonfly, than bury oneself in the sand and live for four hundred years like Ocean Quahog.

As for men, the ones blessed with long life achieve very little in this world. Although Methuselah lived nine hundred and sixty nine years, he did not accomplish anything significant. Jesus Christ, on the other hand, only died in his thirties, yet he changed the entire world.

Longevity does not grant great accomplishments; still, as a man I never felt anything like what I felt when I was vaccinated. As the blessed immunity surged through my blood, all I could think about was the number of years it would add to my life. I felt an overwhelming joy, and I celebrated by jumping around and jumping on Atete's back.

After a while, it occurs to me that this extension of my life is only within a dog's lifespan. My chances of turning back to a human are still quite slim. My joy and celebration soon turns to glumness. I decide to resume my journey home. I will never forget Atete's kindness. She has helped me extend my potentially short dog life. Maybe one day, if I become a man again, I will be able to return this favour. I can imagine how sad she will get when she discovers that I am missing. If she only knew that I am a man in the skin of a dog, she would feel even more sorrow for me.

Nevertheless, I feel the only way I can show her my gratitude now is by staying with her for a few more weeks. Thus, this intense sense of loyalty that I have acquired as a dog delays my journey further.

The day I am going to leave Ziway has finally arrived.
When Atete takes the chain off me in the morning, I
take my last, long look at her. Her mother, who has
been watching us, says sarcastically: 'Oh Atete, you
call this a dog?'

She starts to gather her dress as she walks to the toilet. She continues from inside the toilet: 'You keep feeding a dog which doesn't bark! You fatten it up like a sheep, and yet it's not edible.'

I don't have time to listen to the rest of her talk. I say my goodbyes to Atete with my eyes and leave. As I walk away I start to compose a poem in her honour:

> *Is this a memory that I'd indulge?*
> *Not forsaken like mother's nursing.*
> *Dearly recalled and timely upheld*
> *My dream and yours intertwined.*

Twenty

I have left Ziway, and I am running fast in the direction of Meqi. I am so accustomed to running on four legs, that running on two legs would seem strange. Everything can become familiar, in time. I think adaption is easier for animals than humans. No animal with four legs has to learn to crawl before walking. As soon as they are born, they try to stand. Then they straight away try to walk, however uncoordinated. Then they trot.

Human beings show no such accomplishments. The first thing they do when they are born is cry. Everything else has to be learned gradually. Feeding and excreting seems to come more naturally to babies. But as they grow, they still have to learn to eat solids and learn to hold their pee and poo, and learn to use potties and toilets. Learning to sit, crawl or walk, talk—it takes a much longer development phase.

Social norms contribute to the slow development of humans. If a child's instinct is to use the left hand prominently, society forces her to go against her natural strength and train the weaker hand instead. Once a child masters his mother tongue, he learns to read and write. To learn more subjects, such as maths, physics and chemistry, he may yet have to learn a foreign language. Not only must a child learn how to communicate with others and co-exist with them, he also has to learn a trade to enable him to contribute to his community and earn a living. Thus, learning continues throughout a human's lifetime.

Forever students; humans don't always learn what is good and worthy, but also what is bad and harmful. They learn to lie in order to get their way. If others get hurt on the way—such is life. Even our community elders lie. They sometimes lie for a good cause, such as reconciling two parties, and other times they may do it just to further their own cause.

Religious leaders justify their followers' lies by saying that Satan must have deceived them. So people go on practising lies and justifying them. Sometimes one single lie uttered in time of desperation can have disastrous consequences.

People are mostly the result of nurture. Being born is just the beginning. Apart from practical training, people learn to feel; from how to love, to how to take pride, to malign, to hate, to regret—all is learned. Then it is practised; from betrayal to unshakable faith.

Everything is achieved through process and practice. People change according to circumstances. We can only say what man, through his diligence, has achieved thus far; we don't know what else can be achieved in the future.

I am not reflecting on learning and praxis to make myself accept life as a dog. Yet, I have no guarantee that I would not accept it eventually. At this moment I don't have any guarantee about anything. I don't even have any guarantee that this road I am running on will not give way into an abyss.

I run for about thirty kilometres and reach Meqi town. I think, before I resume with my journey, I need to look for some scraps of food. The town is full of onions. Almost all the trucks I see are overloaded with onions, lumbering along in every direction. I see very few trucks loaded with cabbages or potatoes, the rest are all laden with red onions. Seeing so much red makes me crave meat.

The amount of time I spent searching for food in this town would have been enough to get me to the next town, if I had carried on with my journey. I was about to give up and leave when I saw a puppy running from a backyard with a goat's head. I chased the puppy and snatched his trophy without any difficulty. The pup had no option but sit back and admire the expertise with which I polished the goat's head. Thanks to Atete, now that I'm vaccinated, I no longer have to cower away from other dogs. I recall, after I have finished eating the tongue, the saying that "those who eat goat's tongue will end up talkative." Talkative or not, I just wish I could be a person. I intended to leave a scrap for the pup, but I couldn't resist tearing the ligaments and crushing the bones and, before I knew it, all went into my tum. So much for my intentions about teaching youngsters to share.

I leave Meqi, the town flooded with red onions, and reach a tiny town called Alem Tena. On either side of the main road are stacks of raggedly filled sacks. They are filled with charcoal. There are only a few acacia trees around here. I wonder where they get the wood to make charcoal? I resist the temptation to linger and visit the town. I have to reach Mojo city before nightfall.

I guess it's about thirty kilometres to Mojo. I quicken my pace and reach a market village called Kenter. Casks of red onions and tomatoes line the road begging to be noticed. I must be approaching Koka dam. This abundant harvest must be produced by the rich soil deposits around the reservoir. As I walk a bit further, I come upon the reservoir in full view, fed by the Awash River.

Awash slithers along the rift valley like a python and peacefully gushes into Koka Reservoir. As the river reaches the dam on an open plane, it does not roar or foam with fury. Koka produces over six hundred tonnes of fish a year. There is a variety of birdlife around the lake. However, Koka is gradually under pressure from increasing sediments caused by environmental degradation. The dam is threatened by increasing soil deposits, as the growing human population distresses the country. I silently lament the tragedy of these two badly managed resources; strangling the life from both lake and land.

Any mention of Awash always brings to my mind Laureate Tsegaye Gebremedihin's poem. I feel as if the gentle breeze from the lake is whispering the verses:

> *How long ...... Awash?*
> *Down from Mecha you flood*
> *Red with fertile soil's blood*

Shoa's navel sweats, her streams labour
Your valleys, gorges and rocks splinter
What are you Awash? What makes you ail?
Apart from other waters, are you exceptional?
Made to consume your kin like spiderlings.

I realize I am thirsty, so I go down to the shore to drink. I wash down my thirst, and the verses, with the river water; the life-giver and destroyer.

Beyond the reservoir, some greenhouses are bunched together like a settlement. As I pass through the minor towns of Ijersa and Koka, the aroma of flowers and strawberry farms delights my senses.

From a distance, I see thick black smoke blowing skyward. I must be approaching the industrial city of Mojo. As I walk past a Chinese cement factory, it starts to get dark. I stop to gawk at a billboard advertising Mojo's modern abattoir, as if a piece of meat will drop out of it. This is where Ethiopia's cattle are slaughtered for export. Not only the meat, but also the hide is exported. We then pay a premium for imported leather brands that might have been made from the same hides we exported. Embittered by the irony, I enter the city of Mojo, its stink courtesy of the leather tanning industry. I have no option but to spend the night here. I wish I could block my nose. I can't seem to get used to this foul smell.

The trucks that deliver goods from the Djibouti border are parked for the night all over the city. The drivers lounge around small traditional coffee houses. These coffee houses are considered a cottage industry. Ladies of all ages armed with *jebena*—clay pots—brew fresh coffee to earn money. The aroma from the roasting coffee blends with the smoke of frankincense, toning down the stench from the tannery.

Truck drivers are all over the coffee shops, sipping their coffee. Some of them also indulging in another stimulant; their khat-filled cheeks make them look like they have glandular fever. Women in figure-hugging clothes walk around, chitchatting with the customers. The drivers follow this spectacle with their tired eyes. The women smile back. They sometimes pour coffee, or help sort the khat leaves, whispering 'relax.'

Outspoken customers command the attention of the quiet listeners. Those who are already high on khat wet their lips often with their tongues, like they can't wait to get a taste of something delicious. With their bulging eyes and protruding tongues they look like Māori warriors, but instead of frightening their enemies, they ponder; picking at their teeth. The fragrance of the frankincense is by now overpowered by the stench from the tannery, and the smell of flavoured tobacco blends with it to create an indescribable odour. The hookah smoker has his eyes closed, like a saxophone player playing with a passion. Opening his eyes, he wipes the pipe with his sleeve and passes it on to the next smoker. A madman is begging for khat scraps at the entrance of one coffee house. As he is suffering from withdrawal symptoms, he will take any green leaf that passes for khat.

As fascinating as this bustling scene is, I have to leave and look for leftover food. On my return, I slump in a dark corner and continue to watch the drama for most of the night.

Twenty-One

My journey has become instinctive. As I start to approach Addis Ababa I get more excited. While I traverse the towns of Debre Zeit, Dukem and then Akaki, and Kality... my heart starts to quiver with anxiety. Although the journey from Mojo only took me two days, it felt like an eternity. My mind is completely consumed with thoughts of my family.

When I reach Addis Ababa, every scent I pick up subconsciously reminds me of my wife and children. I stop when I get to Kality prison, nicknamed Alem Bekagn, or "farewell to the world." I can't say what it was; it may have been some kind of intuition that made me halt. Prison guards are posted both at the gate and the watchtower. Sometimes it feels like there are more prisons in Ethiopia than schools. There are prisons in every village, while you can't say the same for schools. There are thousands of prisoners in central prisons like this one. However there are more innocent inmates in there than criminals.

I imagine the prisoners packed in small cells like

sardines. I try to conjure images of the innocents set up and convicted for crimes they never even imagined. The blameless inadvertently made to do time with the petty thief and the murderer. I wish I could go in there and sniff out the innocent from the criminals and set them free. The leaders who wrongly convicted these people know that their only crime was to speak their minds. If they were released, the demoralized public would instinctively hold their heads high, and the weakened muscles of youth would start to pulse with passion.

When I reached Addis Ababa, I felt this dejected spirit and anger in the air. I sense the day of reckoning is not far. It is evident that the majority of the public has a suppressed desire for change. Many have been noting how the greedy leading party and its beneficiaries have been plaiting their own noose for a while.

Even the cadres are tired of the propaganda they've been deafening the public with. The people have watched those in power irresponsibly manipulate the system to rob them blind. Although they use the age-old "tribal politics" to achieve this, which the rest of the world has abandoned, the seemingly slumbering public will soon awaken to ask the dreaded questions. The nagging pain that that the public has been nursing for so long has turned into a stabbing pain that surely will soon become unbearable. Then no power on earth will be able to suppress the tormented public's reaction.

A prison guard hits me with the butt of his rifle and I remember where I am, and what I am. I don't remember getting so close to the prison gate. I don't react fast enough, so he kicks me in the loins. I realize there is nothing I can do for the innocents who are languishing behind that gate. If I stay here any longer I will be beaten to a pulp, so I scamper away and get on with my journey.

I navigate my way through the centre of Addis Ababa and reach Arat Kilo; the palace, which stands on elevated ground in quiet serenity. Nobody seems to steal an admiring glance at it any more. Surrounded by slim eucalyptus trees, it looks more like an agricultural institute than a palace. The deceased Prime Minister's controversial, long-winded orders have dissipated like a cloud scattered by the wind.

Nobody seems to pay heed to the new Prime Minister. Many seem to assume that his authority is not much higher than the palace chef's. The fact that he has no influence is being discussed everywhere. So trying to break into the palace now seems to me a waste of energy, until something noteworthy occurs. The guards at the watchtower are not as vigilant as they used to be; instead they look sleepy.

Out of curiosity I circle around the palace perimeter. The gap between the metal bars of the fence is no larger than twenty-five centimetres. There is no way I can squeeze through there. However, if I still had the inclination to get in, I am sure I would have found another way.

I leave Arat Kilo and carry on walking uphill. I have missed the Piazza area. I walk past Ras Mekonen Bridge and enter the Piazza. Nothing seems to have changed. I carry on uphill to Arada. Here, the lower ground of St. George's church has been razed to lay railway tracks. The public officials are in their usual five-year-cycle of "building up and tearing down." They start a new project without finishing current projects. When asked, 'Why?' they reply: 'To enable the continuation of the development process...' their rehearsed jargon. What an irrelevant answer to a relevant question!

Their track record is proof of their inability to set goals beyond the five-year election period. Roads are built to secure re-election. The fact that they tear down what they built only the previous year shows that they don't have a sustainable national plan or vision.

They tear up a road they built only a year before to lay today's railway tracks. The ring road that they bragged about, until the public was bored, is now partially torn out to make way for rails. It is normal to see construction workers digging up a newly constructed road near election time. 'Why?' The answer today will be to lay telephone cables. At the next election they might say: 'To lay water pipes.' They use these ill-planned projects, which end up wasting public money, to propagandise the image of a progressive leadership. The legendary Ethiopian singer's lyrics resonate well with this experience:

> *Not believing in what they represent*
> *Rather trust their lips than their result*
> *They blend malice with spite*
> *Concealing truth with deceit*

Although the concrete roads they build so often break with the next rainy season, it doesn't stop them from blowing their own trumpets about how productive they are. They brag as if they invest from their personal accounts, rather than public funds. They make it seem like they work from the kindness of their hearts, rather than doing their duty. The tax and excise rates they charge are not practical. Consequently, tens of thousands of citizens legally and illegally migrate out of the country every year.

A few years ago, the young women that worked in most urban cafés looked like elegant airline steward-esses. Most of those women have now gone to the Middle East to work as housemaids for better wages. It would be typical of government officials to report this trend thus: 'Due to the favourable conditions that the government has created, thousands of young women have been promoted from employment in the local service industries and are investing their remittances.'

The fact that most of these women were forced to work abroad because of the meagre local wages and high living costs would not be mentioned. It is impos-sible to hope for anything good these days. Dreams of an improved standard of living, by any legal means, are hopeless. Hoping for a better leadership is useless when there is but one party. Even hoping to find a dependable, trustworthy man is unrealistic. The politi-cal leadership have put this whole society into a stupor. They have dragged standards down to the pits. With the high incidence of imprisonment for anyone who challenges the leadership, courage and resistance have gone down the drain. Instead they recruit vagrants and greedy opportunists to be their henchmen.

Ah, these thoughts are a welcome distraction from my anxiety about my family. By the time I get to Gedam neighbourhood it is getting dark. The traffic is starting to slow down a bit. I can hear the dogs in the area barking here and there. It is uncanny how they stop barking and restart almost in unison. They seem organized. It seems like the political leaders' scheme, to organize a spy for every group of five, may have drifted to include dogs as well. Joking aside, the leaders have become expert at organizing spying, down to a community and even family level—a perfect system to divide and rule. I wonder if my wife has become a spy?

My house is located behind the Central Investigation Bureau. Of the other houses in the area, mine looks grandest. The brick wall around my house is built high and it is fortified by barbed wire. The inner compound has leafy trees and beautiful flowers. As I get closer to the house my panting increases.

I stop in front of the closed gate, gasping for more air. My fur stands high on my skin as an indescribable feeling goes through my body. I can't hear anything from the house. All is quiet. I wonder if my wife has remarried? How about my children... I hope nothing bad has happened to them.

Twenty-Two

I curl and lie down at the corner of the gate. My body is exhausted by the long trek. My paws feel tender from traversing towns on hot concrete roads.

Midnight is approaching. The frequent lightning indicates that a storm is brewing. Where do I shelter? The high walls of my house make jumping in impossible. The fence I built against intruders is keeping me from sheltering in my own house.

Human suffering arises from the boundaries they themselves have set up; the walls they build around, and the complexities they weave for themselves. Such are life's tragedies, boundaries based on race, religion, ideology, and philosophy—fortified by seemingly magical walls. This is what the wall I built around my house is telling me; making me sleep outside.

Brrr, I'm so cold,
Can it be this chilly...

The lyrics from the old song ring in my ears, along with the frosty wind. How I long for my wife's warm embrace! How is this possible? I'm a dog and she is a beautiful lady. The gap between us exceeds the evolutionary divide between man and ape. The distance that separates us is not physical—it cannot be measured in yards. It is so vast that it is beyond measurement. She is human and I, a dog. We function differently. She can articulate herself with speech and a pleasant voice. I cannot. She doesn't even like my sort! If I ever get near her, she will come for me with a club.

I was purposely indulging in warm thoughts about my wife to ward off the cold, but I snap out of this dream world when I hear a car approaching. Who could be coming to my house this late into the night?

It pulls right up to the gate, the front lights beaming straight into my eyes. I think I recognize the car. I try to make out the number plate. Sure, I know exactly whose car this is. It belongs to the person I hate most in this world. The owner of this white Mercedes is none other than the cruel Qelemintos Ture.

He befriended me many years ago, only to rip me off. I can't think of anyone who is more capable at disguising his filthy intentions. He is very convincing. At one time, he was a very successful broker abroad. Soon after I came back from my overseas studies, I invested all my savings into starting up a business. Qelemintos was introduced to me through a friend, and bought a share in my company.

About a year later, he cunningly tempted my loyal employees to go to bigger companies and recommended me to hire his own people. By the time I realized his crafty schemes, it was too late. My business was as empty as a hive abandoned by its bees.

I lost fifty-six million birr. He cried his crocodile tears over the loss, patted me on the back, and left me high and dry. Later on, I heard that with the money he siphoned from me, he established another business and bought three tower blocks in Addis Ababa. I took him to court on fraud charges, for which he was imprisoned. However, within six months, he managed to pull some strings and get himself released. That is when I realized that he was well connected. He can pull strings as he pleases, among the Police, the judges and even politicians. That's when I vowed to leave him alone and let the God of Vengeance take over.

I may have left him alone, but now I see he is not through with me. Here he is, parked by my gate in the dead of night. He must have heard about how my car was found abandoned in the South and assumed I was dead. Has he come to celebrate?

People who've heard about how he swindled me nick-named him "Mento," after the kitchen implement—a metal rod, with a hook at the end, for taking out meat from a boiling cooking pot. I also stopped using his real name back then. I can't actually say his name, the very mention of it sends shivers through me. Mento's hands are like the devil's. He would delve into volcanic embers with his hooks to salvage anything desirable. If he saw gold coins thrown from a cliff, he would jump to grab them. He wouldn't think about falling, only the riches. *Mento, Mento, Mento!* Why is he at my gate in the middle of the night? What is he trying to hook out this time, I wonder?

I hear loud laughter coming from the car. I recog-nize his laugh. His fake, boisterous laugh cackles on for a long time. He never laughs out of good cheer; it is always out of sarcasm or amusement, at best. It feels like the devil himself has become amused at my expense. I get up and approach the car.

The car stereo is playing soft, romantic music. The smell of whiskey wafts from the car as Mento lowers the window on his side. He gulps whiskey from the bottle and passes it to the woman next to him. She does the same.

Their laughter is getting louder as they whisper to each other. Although his laughter almost overpowers hers, I think I recognize it. I walk around the car to her side. Through the dim light her even, white teeth shine out. I think I recognize those teeth... and those rosy lips. She briefly looks in my direction. I know that look!

I see her shapely thigh through the wide, gaping slit of her black dress. She has draped one leg over Mento's. A sudden flash of lightning enables me to see her properly.

It is my wife, Ephrata! I feel like that lightning bolt struck me. I wish it had struck me dead! I wish the very ground I stand on would split in two and swallow me. I feel sluggish. My head wobbles—too heavy for my neck to support it. I wish the wild beasts in the woods had ended my life. I wish the vultures of the rift valley had gouged my eyes out. I feel like poison has been injected into my bloodstream. I stagger and fall. I take a few breaths to brace myself and rise again. They are still passing the bottle to each other and chugging down the whiskey. A bit later, they get closer to each other as if drawn by a magnet. My wife reaches her other leg beyond the handbrake and around Mento's waist. He encloses her with his big arm, and pushes out his over-sized chin towards her face. Then he lands his chunky lips on her delicate ones.

In the lustful frenzy that follows they do not even notice the liquor bottle that falls, spilling some of its contents. She unbuttons his shirt and leans on his bushy chest. He in turn unzips her dress, unhooks her bra, and starts squeezing her boobs.

Another shock courses through my body as I witness the car being rocked up and down, but this time I manage just to sit on my haunches and not fall over. After what seems like an eternity to me, the car stops moving. They hurriedly adjust their clothes and empty what is left of the whiskey. Having composed themselves, they start to giggle, breaking the brief silence that followed.

'How did I do Epha?' he asks, shortening her name affectionately.

'Do you have to ask...? *Kikiki... kikiki*,' she giggles. 'You were amazing. This time was particularly incredible.'

I realize from her reply that they didn't have sex for the first time tonight.

'It's crazy to be doing this at our gate... when we're

only a few steps away from our bed… crazy,' they giggle in unison.

The shameless phrases he uses: "our gate," and "our bed," finally confirming the dreaded marital union between my wife and my mortal enemy.

'*Kikiki…* daring to do something unusual, adventurous sometimes can add flavour to life's boring routine,' she says approvingly.

'I… suspect you used to do such unusual things with your previous husband as well.'

Is he loath to call me by my name? Woe to me, for my name has become despicable!

'Well… not in a car… but we did do it in a park in Barcelona, when we were on a holiday in Spain… but I won't tell you how we did it then.'

'What is there to hide about it, my darling? Tell me.'

'It's embarrassing! I won't tell you. Oh, I'll never forget the time we did it in a vineyard in Milan, when we visited Italy. Also, in Argentina… Buenos Aires… that was unforgettable.' She hides her face with her palms. 'We mostly did it in the woods on our travels. I don't know, maybe he had some kind of forest fetish. Forget about him—these special moments that I have with you are the ones I want to remember. They're as good as the memories I have of him. Now, I need to relish this moment… *kikiki,*' she giggles again.

'*Ha ha ha…*' hesitantly, he joins in with the laughter.

'This is a new chapter. Don't remind me of him. His chapter is closed. Maybe some serpent gobbled him up when he was roaming in the woods that he loved so much. I bet even the serpent forgot about him soon enough, and continued its search for another meal.'

'A serpent? Now, that is unlikely. What I think is that, in his greed, he had a business feud with someone who ended up murdering him. Money is the downfall of the greedy.'

'Please stop reminiscing about the long-dead in this darkness. Why tonight anyway? We haven't talked about him for ages. You can't possibly be jealous of the dead! Don't you recall what we used to do, even when he was alive? We could talk of the times when we all travelled together, and we managed to get away from him and make out…. Pass me the bottle, if there's any left.'

'My goddess of love, whoever worships you would be jealous! *Ha ha ha…*' He holds her close. Compliant, she leans on his shoulders.

'We better get inside. It's starting to drizzle again.'

'Did you love him?'

'No more than I love you.'

'What does that mean?' he asks in a stern voice.

'Didn't I ask you to drop this nonsense?' She straightens up. 'Who asked you to investigate the standard of my love, anyway? To tell you the truth, I never really loved him. We met... I liked the way he made me feel... so, I didn't need to look elsewhere... then... I accidentally got pregnant... I had his child. Again I got pregnant without planning to, and we had our second child. We had a happy family for a while, until I met you. Now he is dead and we are together—end of story. Please don't ask me such questions—ever again.'

I cannot witness any more betrayal, or bear to listen to more deceit. My ears are ringing, as if they've been punched. The rain drowns their voices out. Mento starts the engine and honks. The guard immediately opens the gate. I think about dashing into the compound behind the car, but my legs feel like they are glued to the ground. I can't move. I watch the gate closing again. I can't even feel the downpour upon me. I only smell the stench steaming from my body, so hot that even the rain fails to cool me.

I can feel the venom of hate coursing through every vein in my body. I feel like I am going to explode. I let the rain drench me until it runs out.

The flood, draining, carries all kinds of garbage down the roadside. I finally start to feel the numbing effect of the cold in my bones. The venom that was boiling my blood now seems to have chilled and congealed.

I scurry down to Dejach Wube neighbourhood to find a corner to curl up in. I can't find a single dry corner. I take the road on the left and head towards Arada and Saint George's church. I am just hoping to get inside the church and shelter there, when I remember what I am. A dog is never allowed to enter church grounds lest it will desecrate them. If one happens to cross the bounds, then someone will surely chase it away, or even worse, give it a severe blow. Only humans are fit to enter; though sinners to the core, they are still considered cleaner than the likes of me.

I walk closer to the plastic shelters of the homeless, who are sleeping huddled together for warmth. Although the flood is leaking through their bedding, they insist on remaining asleep. If they awoke, the glaring reality would be too grim to bear. To see the light of dawn they must patiently let the night pass, however uncomfortable their bed is. I curl up next to them.

Twenty-Three

Unable to sleep a wink, I see the first rays of dawn breaking through the city's skyline. I wonder if the old saying is true: "if you touch dog shit and rub your eyes, then you'll never sleep a wink."

I haven't had a single good night's sleep since I became a dog. The Eastern horizon is glowing brighter. The jangling of the Church bells has already woken the homeless beggars, who jostle for position—stretching out their palms for alms. The faint chirping of sparrows is only just audible through the destinations shouted across the taxi rank.

I start the new day with a burning desire for vengeance. Even though I am a dog, I have shared my desire for vengeance with Saint George, who helped our people fight the battle of Adwa against the invading Italian forces. Unless the holy Saint intercedes on my behalf for healing, the spear of vengeance that pierced my heart will take more than one lifetime to mend.

But I will not attempt to seek vengeance in my present state. I must turn back into a human. I have to see with human eyes the sacrifice they will make to atone for the pain they have inflicted upon me. I have to witness with human eyes their terror, trembling with such fright that they wish for death. Unless they see me, the person they have betrayed, then my vengeance would be meaningless. I plan to execute this with great care. It has to be as cruel as their infidelity. My revenge will have them curse their carefree transgressions. It will make their mocking laughter resound in their ears.

I have not made any definite plans yet. Prior to that I need to address the difficult task of returning to humanity. It takes one tiny mistake to degrade oneself from respectability and become a pariah. To be evil is easier than to be saintly. It is easier to hate than love. To destroy is easier than to build. To preserve the status quo is easier than making progress. I remember the spell that changes one into a dog so well:

> **ELAS ELAS ELAS**
> **UHLA UHLA UHLA**
> **KAMOS KAKAMOS AKAKAMOS ELA**

I memorised a spell that takes hours to cast. What I failed to do was memorize the reversing spell. The scroll they are both written upon is in my house, locked inside a chest. This house, however, no longer belongs to me. It now belongs to my enemy. By now they might have got rid of the chest.

If that is the case, I will forever remain a dog. If not, I may have a slight chance of retrieving the scroll. I better concentrate on that remote chance. Hope is a powerful thing. Without a flicker of hope one cannot survive a single day in harsh circumstances. I have to go to the house.

I take the narrow road up the Dejach Wube neighbourhood, towards my house. The gate is closed. I guess they are still inside. Maybe husband and wife are still in bed, in each other's arms? Maybe they are still nursing the hangover from last night? There is nothing to get them out of bed early, anyway. They won't have any anxieties to rouse them from their slumber. Why would they rise in the morning to work, when they have so much of my wealth to squander? Or maybe they are worrying about which holiday destination to choose next?

Her casual words ring in my ears, saying, "I accidentally got pregnant and had his child." Her voice is no longer sweet and melodic. It is the screeching hiss of a snake.

I wonder how those *accidental* children of mine are doing? Have they lost weight? Have they been neglected? Has their evil stepfather been scolding them; bulging his red eyes to scare them into submission?

With these thoughts in mind, I wait by the closed gate for most of the morning. Then, with the ignition of a car engine, the gate abruptly swings open. Without a moment's hesitation I slip in unnoticed. Attired in sport's gear, the master of the house is working out. His distended belly wobbles like an Ethiopian priest's drum, slung from the neck to perform songs of praise. As he skips a rope, his belly flaps up and down; doing push-ups it almost touches the ground.

I stand by a corner and continue to watch this hilarious scene. My amusement soon turns to grief when I notice my children sitting on the steps. They are hiding their heads between their knees. I wonder what's wrong with them? They are still in their nightwear. Their necks and legs seem very thin. Their entire frame seems skinnier than I remember.

'Hey you two!' Mento shouts at them. 'Aren`t you going to school?'

They both look up, as startled as thieves caught stealing.

'T-t-t-today is Sunday...' my daughter stammers.

This toad doesn't even know which day of the week it is, I think. Why should he keep track of time? When it so favours him.

'Aren't you at least going to wash your faces? I don't want a swarm of flies to follow you into the house. You better get up and wash yourselves right now!'

While eavesdropping on people in the South, I was amused to hear people scoff at a government report that 'the number of flies in the cities has decreased.' Mento must not have heard. If he had, he wouldn't dare to contradict his high-powered friends.

'Why are you still here?' he shouts, breathing heavily.

'Th... There is no water,' they answer in unison.

I think to myself: so much for all the progress his government friends boast about, while drinking their whiskey at night.

'No water? Go and fetch some from the next block, then. Get on with it—now!'

They quickly get up and head to the gate, fetching two big jerry cans.

'Hey, Mero!' he shouts to the guard. 'Why on earth did you let this stray dog in?'

The guard fumbles out from his hut, holding a club. I dash out of the gate faster than him, following on the heels of my children. He closes the gate right behind me. Had I been a tad slower, my own faithful guard would have clubbed me. Oh how prompt he used to be to obey my orders and please me—well that was in another lifetime. Normally Mero would not beat a dog, not even a stray one. He loves dogs—but he had to obey his new, cruel master.

I follow my children and watch them return, staggering with their heavy load. My heart bleeds for them, but I can't help them. If only they knew the black dog following them was their father! No, they should never find that out! I have to change back into a man and rescue my children from this misery. How though... *how?*

Twenty-Four

I continue gazing eagerly at the gate, which stays firmly closed throughout the afternoon. If the intensity of one's gaze could communicate a wish, the gate would have flung open by now. Anguish wrings my heart whenever I recall my wife's deceit. I don't think I can ever trust a woman again. Well, as the saying goes, "once bitten, twice shy."

How did she manage to deceive me all these years? How could I have been so blind to the secrets she harboured in her heart? I don't believe her heart has only four chambers. If doctors were to examine it, I think they would find several more crammed with secrets and desires. She is like a cat, soft and always craving affection. When given love she purrs and appears content, yet never weak—she can pounce at any displeasure. I wonder if all women are like that?

In my present state, I picture a woman to be like the stomach of a cow or goat, composed of several muscular sacs. This is the image I conjure up. God the creator may liken them to a heart, or a kidney. A sculptor may represent womankind in gold, a precious metal that shifts its form in the flames. The way we conceive of the world is through our experience; a subjective lens. Maybe someone who has not gone through what I have will detest my view. Perhaps, understandably, he sees women through the same lens he sees his own mother. I for one believe my mother has no gender. A woman who has been wronged by men may think of me badly, because I am a male dog. Men like Mento have also wronged me. It is important to tell the difference between behaviour and nature. Behaviour is nurtured. One adopts it from the way one is raised, by family and society.

I agonize about these things because I have been hurt. Matters concerning the love of a woman, or one's nation, can be gravely worrying. Both are complex. Both can be likened to the stomach of a ruminant, with many sacs to store their secrets and complexities. To think about these is to endure endless anxiety.

The woman who was my wife, only a year ago, is now Mento's wife. My country, which was once Soviet Russia's ally, has befriended the United States. My wife may be cheating on me while she still embraces me in her arms at night. In the same way, my country can imprison me and silence me to advance the interests of outsiders.

One cannot predict if and when your woman or your country will turn their back on you. When Emperor Tewodros II was about to take his life in Mekdela, the whole of Ethiopia, from mother to priest, had turned their backs on him.

Our Motherland's heart is slippery. Her loyalty shifts with whoever rules her. Mother Ethiopia is split into Eritrea and Ethiopia. The country's borders once included Egypt, Nubia, Yemen, and even extended as far as Madagascar. Now it is a different story. We don't even know if the current rulers have the country's best interests at heart.

Mento honks from inside for the guard to open the gate for him. This time he is driving my car. His wife is sitting in the front seat. I wonder where they are going, dressed formally like this? Maybe they are going to a banquet? Maybe people will get up from their seats to greet them? They look pretty respectable when seen from the outside. I can see he is wearing my tie, the expensive one I bought in Paris. He is even wearing my cologne. My favourite scent drifts to me from the cracked window.

Traditionally the clothes of the deceased are donated to the poor, except precious heirlooms, which are kept to pass on to future generation. People like Mento are immune to culture and tradition. They are happy to plunder hard-working people, so why not a deceased one?

My dog nature urges me to follow them. I follow the car, inhaling the exhaust fumes, barking.

'Woof... woof... woof! Woof... woof... woof...' I wish I could denounce them, instead of barking.

The other dogs in the village hear my barking and join in. When we get close to the police station, other dogs join the chase. I feel like my fellow dogs are supporting me in my pleas for justice. However, what good is noise in a country where dishonesty reigns? If making noise were enough to demolish this monumental wall of deceit, then I would lead all the dogs of the city in a barking frenzy.

The government seems to use language, not as a means of communication, but to divide the public along ethnic lines. That may be the reason why the People's pleas mean nothing to them. So, this is a change of tack, barking for justice! I stop chasing the car and start barking at the police station. The other dogs, again, follow suit. At this point, I wonder if the guards are reminded of the song, *Who let the dogs out?* As I am closest to the gate, one of the guards reaches out and hits me on my chin with the butt of his rifle.

Realising this is not going to work, I give up and sprint in the direction of my house, before the other dogs can become inquisitive about who I am. As I suspected, the pack pursues me. A dog with patchy fur jumps on me. Had I not been vaccinated, I wouldn't have dared to fight back. Although I feel awful biting a dog, I bite the poor thing in several places. Loath as I am to add to this pitiful dog's misery, I need to scare off the rest of the pack.

Dogs by nature need to know who is in charge. I made my point clear; the others stop in their tracks and bark half-heartedly. All the dogs in this pack are scrawny. Leftover food is no longer thrown away in this city. These days people don't even have enough for themselves, let alone scraps of meat to throw away. Leftover food from events and hotels is sent to the market, nowadays. There are stalls in Merkato that sell a handful of leftover food for one Birr. If these dogs knew this, they would give up hope in humans, become feral and flee to the woods.

These days loyalty is no longer deemed a virtue. So dogs and their loyal nature are of little use. Duplicity, on the other hand, is very useful for success in this society. In this sense, unlike dogs, cats are in luck, as they are fickle and more amenable to duplicity. If being a cat can be considered fortunate, then the cats found in the kitchens of every Ministry are surely to be envied. In the past, these creatures were on hand to reap benefits from the invading Italians. Then they were on the front line to welcome the returning Emperor when the Italians were defeated. Oddly enough, they were also found stirring up the mob when the same Emperor was deposed, shouting out: 'Dog, you are a dog.'

The same creatures helped the Communist government that took power, slaughtering the bright generation of youths who challenged it. Years later, when the rebels succeeded in chasing out the Communist leader and took over the abandoned palace, the treacherous cats were already waiting in kitchen.

Unfortunately, eliminating these creatures is impossible because of their cunning nature. When time favours them, they act like lions. When their cover is blown they become hard to track, like tigers. Woe to the hunter who manages to track such a treacherous cat, for he will end up being the bleeding prey.

Most of the dogs have now calmed down. The only dog that still seems angry sees a passing cat and chases after it. Noting my victory over the pack, I turn away from them and start to walk gracefully, like a lion, back towards my house.

Twenty-Five

A few days go by while I wait for the chance to slip into my house and search for the magic scrolls. All the while, my wife and Mento seem to be having the time of their lives.

I still burned with jealousy for the first couple of days. Those who have gone through it will know how toxic it is. I don't think anyone is capable of describing the exact feeling. As amazing as language is in communicating feelings, in circumstances like this it falls lamely short. A deep exhalation, as if to blow out a candle, moaning—these seem to describe the feeling better than words. The day I fell in love, I remember I likened it to heaven and stopped wishing for anything better. When I started to feel jealous, I saw a glimpse of hell and stopped dreading it.

In ancient religious manuscripts, a damned person is said to burn in the fires of hell not once, but multiple of times. The burnt skin seems to be replaced by a new one only to be burned again. The pain is afresh, as new, every time.

This is kind of how I felt the last few days. My skin was itching all over, and no amount of scratching could bring me any relief. Of all those bitter days, today seems slightly less bitter.

Mento and my wife—his wife, I mean—left early in the morning. My children also left for school. Mero the guard, who has eagerly been waiting for this, is going to the service quarters to make love to the maid. He is in such a hurry, he hasn't shut the gate properly. As he dashes to the backyard, I slip into the compound and push the gate shut.

As I step into the living room, I hear noises from the bedroom. Mero and the maid are talking about their fantasy of trying out their masters' bed.

'No Mero, not here.'

'Come on, I'm telling you they won't come back anytime soon.'

'That may be so... but what about the perfume sprayed on the bed? What if they smell it on us?'

'Since when do people spray perfume on their bed?'

'Go on, smell it.'

I imagine Mero bending down to smell the bed.

'There... you're worry for nothing. This is only their natural scent, not perfume.'

'Well... what if our scent replaces theirs?'

179

'We will just shake it out, come on...'

'Oh you foolish man... since when can you shake off a scent, like dust?'

I can sense from their tone that they are both dying to make love on that dream bed. Mero doesn't realize that the maid wants it just as bad, she just doesn't want to take responsibility.

'No Mero... What if...'

'Remember, they didn't find out last time.'

'We were lucky that time... They came back so drunk that they wouldn't have noticed anything...'

'Trust me, they will come back just as drunk today!'

'You sound like you took them out for drinks at the Hilton... Imagine that!'

'Maybe one day fortune will smile on me...'

He then starts to sing an out-of-tune love song to her with his congested voice. She laughs with genuine amusement.

'Do you really think our luck will turn for the better?'

'One day... Now you turn this way!'

The banter stops. They must be otherwise engaged. I start looking around the sitting room. Almost everything is as it was when I lived here. The only thing that has changed is the photos hung on the wall. All my photos are replaced by Mento's. The frames are the same. My wife's smile, and the way she looked up into my eyes is exactly the same, only Mento is in my place. She was always photogenic.

The next two frames hold their engagement and wedding photos. I notice a couple of the bridesmaids and the groom's best men were also witnesses at our wedding. I feel nauseous. I move my eyes to the next picture: their honeymoon, by the sea, on a tropical island. I leave off and make my way to the study.

This room looks like it hasn't been used in a long while. It is dusty and covered with cobwebs. It smells of damp and mildew. Shelves full of books cover every wall. Of all my belongings in this house, these books are the most precious to me. To Mento and his wife however, they mean nothing. For them, knowledge is something only fools would spend time pursuing.

As I go about, looking for the chest that I left here, I hear the hooting of a car outside the gate. How annoying! I dart out of the study and stumble upon Mero, who is rushing out of the bedroom. My sharp nose immediately picks up the smell of fresh semen about him. He looks flustered. He trips over his own trousers twice while trying to fasten them. Although we were almost face-to-face, he hasn't noticed me. As he rushes to the gate, I hide in the garden.

In my hiding place, I start waiting for nightfall. It seems like the sun will not set. The saying, "a fool's day never sets," was coined to suggest that a fool cannot tell night from a day. However, to someone yearning for the sun to set, it also never seems to do so. It feels like my desire for the night to come is actually keeping it aloft.

Twenty-Six

I stay in the garden for three days. Not a single chance to get into the house and find the magic scrolls. Fortunately no one ventured into the garden. Well, apart from a fat rat, which ended up being my lunch. I also caught a sparrow, but I set it free out of pity. I don't know upon which moral grounds I chose to free the sparrow and eat the rat. Oh, I also can't deny that I devoured the dead cockerel I found beside the bush. I couldn't tell if it died of a disease or some other cause, but hunger knows no such qualms. I am still alive and well, that is what matters.

I may get lucky tonight. I notice the back door is ajar. Keleb, the maid, has gone into the guard's hut. The master and mistress of the house seem to have retired to their bedroom. I take this chance to slip in and head for the study.

I can hear Mento snoring in the bedroom, but I am still wary of being found out. I can't wait to find the scroll and change back to my human self.

Excitement can sometimes stand in the way of success. A combination of positive thinking and hard work seem to be the key to success. I have seen people stumble, just before achieving their goal, because of their zeal.

I feel comfort in the knowledge that Mento's loud snore will disguise any noise I may make while searching for the scroll. Let him snore! After all, he has no worries in this world, having taken over my wealth and my beautiful wife. Let the lord of this household snore in his blissful sleep!

I start searching for the chest in every corner. While sniffing it out, I accidentally touch a pile of books that come tumbling down. I panic, as if my life is over, pausing to listen out for anyone who has heard the noise. There is nothing.

I clamber out from the scattered pile and continue my search. I notice the chest wedged behind a small shelf. I remember leaving it locked. Now I see it is left ajar. I see that they have taken out my bankbooks and the deeds to the house, but the scrolls are still there. While looking for the shape-shifting spells in particular, from among the thirteen scrolls, I am reminded of how they were first recovered.

It was 1952, and Emperor Haile Selassie commissioned an archaeological team. While they were carrying out a series of excavations around Adwa and Axum, they discovered various cultural artefacts. These artefacts are still on display at the National Museum of Ethiopia. Apart from these, however, other valuable items were also found and their existence kept secret.

My father was a member of this team. He personally found these scrolls among some of the artefacts and chose to keep them a secret. When I grew older, he encouraged me to learn about the mysteries of the ancient world. Following his advice I studied Archaeology in Germany. I obtained my postgraduate degrees in Anthropology and Philology in France and England.

Of all the studies I have done, however, I have dedicated most of my time to acquiring magic and knowledge of the occult. Having a wide network in the field, my father introduced me to renowned Sudanese and Egyptian experts. The more I travelled and learned about these arts, the deeper my curiosity became.

My quest led me to many countries in the Arabian Peninsula, as far as the Persian Gulf. I investigated why the ancient wisdom and knowledge, now considered mere illusion and myth, is dying away.

Ethiopian wizards used to take part in the annual sorcery competition in ancient Egypt. The story of how Akilas, the Ethiopian magician and scholar, won one of these competitions is recorded in writing.

According to this story, Akilas quietly observed the different sorceries until it was his turn. Then he bowed courteously to the Pharaoh and turned to the spectators: 'We have witnessed what the Egyptian Wizards are able to perform. We have also seen the wisdom and art of those who come from Babylon. I will now perform all of the amazing acts conjured thus far, and more,' he claimed, gracefully walking back and forth upon the stage.

Most spectators muttered in disbelief, loudly expressing their doubts. Some even laughed and jeered. Akilas waited until the noise had died down and said, 'If I fail to conjure any of the sorceries performed so far, let me be beheaded before the great and just Pharaoh.'

All fell deadly quiet as the seriousness of the claim sank in. Finally, the Pharaoh accepted the wager and gave consent for Akilas to start his performance.

Just as the other Wizards had done, Akilas quickly shape-shifted into a huge python. As the crowd started to squirm with nervousness he changed back into his human form again. He was greeted with generous applause. He then changed into a raging flame, then to water, then to clouds, then to a strong wind that almost threatened to uproot the marquee....

Akilas finished his performance and bowed down. The awe and cheers from the crowd was unstoppable. Even the Pharaoh applauded enthusiastically.

'All you have seen me perform so far has been done by others,' said Akilas, once the applause had subsided. 'What I am about to show you, however, cannot be done by another.' Next, he took out a sealed scroll from his cloak and claimed that he could read what was inside without opening it.

'You could have memorized the contents,' said the King, unimpressed.

'My Lord, I give you my word that I have never opened or read from this scroll before. If you doubt it my Lord, I can read any other scroll from your own collections, held in your own good hands. The King ordered for some of his most secretly kept scrolls to be unearthed from their hidden place and brought to him. Akilas read each one of them without opening them. No other sage or wizard could do what he did.

After the banquet that was given to celebrate his victory, a camel and accompanying guards were provided for his return journey. Akilas thanked the King for everything he had provided for him, but instead of accepting the official escort, he summoned a bunch of clouds in the clear blue sky. The clouds descended upon Akilas and engulfed him. Thus he made his way back to Ethiopia, carried by the clouds.

Unfortunately, way before there was any chance someone might take a balanced view of this ancient wisdom, a number of wars were intentionally waged against such knowledge.

When Westerners arrived in the continent, as missionaries and colonizers, they brought great destruction upon the wisdom, by ridiculing the art and defaming or executing those who practised it. So many priceless manuscripts were blindly burned. Many that survived the flames were looted away. Now, the real sages are gone and only the witch doctors are left. Pretending to know the art, they tend to deceive uneducated peasants.

Although the ancient world's wisdom is long forgotten and buried, ancient cities have been discovered under oceans. Magnificent and complex buildings have been unearthed in deserts considered uninhabitable by humankind. However, a record of the knowledge behind such technological advancements has not be unearthed.

Throughout the world, there are a few gifted people with paranormal abilities. Researchers have discovered that there are strange phenomena that happen to only one percent of the population.

Beyond the visible world there is an invisible, parallel world with hidden "power of words"—magic.

To a Christian, the biblical quotes "the word became flesh," and, "thou shall eat the fruit of your lips," are familiar. God created the heavens and the earth as well as all things visible and invisible, except for human beings, by the Word.

The poet knows that only when the right words fall in the right verse, to express the right idea, can he become who he is; a poet.

If a politician makes a convincing speech with well-versed words, then he will no doubt get a seat in parliament. He knows that if he speaks about the right things, at the right time, at the right place, to the right crowd, using the right words, then he will win the vote of the people—unless it is rigged.

Words can make one hate, or win another's love. Words can bring one success or failure. With words one can achieve anything. Words can enable one to do anything. Words are the key to everything. This key, however, can unlock both good and evil.

Magic is none other than this; a set of terms and names—arrangements of sundry words. These are words with the ability to forge a connection with the power of nature, not mere cliché.

The words we speak reveal who we are. What we say can cause someone offence or earn us respect. I have come to fully realize the impact words can have on my life. I tell my story, not because I want to initiate people into occult practices, rather, here I want to remind the reader of my earlier warning. In this story I am narrating my life as a dog, parts of the spell that changed me into a dog were stated. I will not be held responsible for any consequence that reading these magic words aloud may cause. I want the reader to understand something very important; the power of words. You can use them for good or evil. Seasoned and kind words can make one's life wonderful, while distasteful and cruel words can be shattering.

Of the Old Testament characters, the Bible specifies which ones had mystic wisdom. Adam and Eve's first two sons were Abel and Cain. Cain killed Abel, and God banished him into a life of wandering. Adam and Even then had another son, Seth. From then on, sons and daughters of Adam were divided into two groups—the clans of Seth and the clans of Cain. Seth's clan lived by thanksgiving and making offerings to God, while Cain's clans fled to live further afield.

Cain's clan studied nature and used herbal medicines to heal the wounds dealt in their wandering lives. To fight off their enemies they shaped metals into swords, spears, knives and arrows. They studied the stars and the elements of nature for optimal productivity. They created arts, which they designed to fashion their clothes and beautify their body.

Seth's clan was attracted to the advancements of Cain's folk and eventually the two merged. This angered God. He vowed to destroy them by an historic flood, saving Noah's family. From Noah's surviving family, the daughters-in-law salvaged the mystic wisdom and practices of Cain's clan and passed them on to their descendants.

The Reayit family line was particularly known for being scholars of the highest order in mystic knowledge. The Kush, who later settled in the Northern part of Ethiopia, are descendants of the Reayits.

It is historically recorded that Moses learnt the practice of the occult from the Kush. When Egyptian sorcerers changed their sticks to snakes, Moses did the same and so much more. The difference was, God blessed his abilities and gave him spiritual power, while others wilfully mastered their power from the Universe.

Today, the modern world continues to invent, experiment and pursue disciplines founded by their forefathers, Cain and his clan, but they choose to neglect or even destroy the mystic aspect of their ancestors.

One such destruction was recorded in the Bible in the Acts of the Apostles. It relates that many magicians burned their books because they converted to Christianity. The account estimates the value of the books burned, in the currency of the day, at 50,000 dinars. Since then, unknown numbers of books have been burned in various countries.

If only the people who chose to destroy this knowledge had cared to investigate, they would have seen that it could have been put to good use. Just as something as simple as herbs, or advanced as nuclear power can be used for good or evil, so can occult knowledge.

Magic can be divided into two categories; black and white. While white magic is used for good uses, the black is used for evil deeds. As fire and water can be used for good or destruction, so can magic be used for either.

It would be easy for me to use my occult knowledge to harm Mento, who robbed me of all my earthly possessions and is right now snoring in the embrace of my wife. However, I choose not to use my powers for evil and lower myself to his level. Whether I shoot him in the head with a pistol, or make him suffer with black magic; either method will involve Cain and his descendant's mastery of natural chemicals and elements. However, the former is used more often in this day and age, and may seem a more acceptable method than the latter.

I should not bother about the method of my vengeance until later. What is important now is to find the means of reclaiming my human form.

After shuffling the scrolls for some time, I eventually find the scroll I desperately need. I hold it between my teeth and leave through the back door.

Twenty-Seven

I hide myself in the garden once again and spread the scroll open. I skim through the artfully transcribed magic words and find the part that changed me into a dog. My heart races with anticipation. Where is the reverse spell? I feel tense with worry. My impatience makes concentration difficult.

I find some other spell that shifts one from human to Python. It is brief:

> AZAHIL KIRSUBAEL
>
> AKRABITIS BERSEYUM
>
> SHADKAEL MEGRIPA
>
> SHADKAEL TOVER

Below is the reverse spell:

> AWRODROS AKRADROEL
>
> TAYASKRODIROEL

I still cannot locate the reversing spell that changes from dog to human. I know very well that the scrolls I left behind in the study had no spells to change one from a dog to human form. For a long while I stay where I am, contemplating my options. Then I panic. *Am I going to live out the rest of my life as a four-legged animal?*

I start thinking about what makes humans stand out from other animals and try to work out what I lack right now, which humans have.

Humans are different because they can learn from their past and improve their lot. Perhaps Ethiopians are the exception in this regard? Although their history dates back thousands of years, they don't seem to have learned much from it. They wage war over the same things that impeded their progress in the past.

There is no significant difference between the dog of today or the one that lived a hundred years ago. The dog of three generations passed had nothing to bequeath to its descendants except its genetic makeup and breed.

What part of being human appeals to me so much that I am obsessed with reversing into that form? Why do I want to become human at a time when humans are changing into beasts? Animals have an instinctive love for their young or their master, which is better than the pretence that is abundant among humans. Animals never pretend to love you. Humans in contrast, may cunningly be plotting each other's demise while they hug and kiss. Their betrayal still feels freshly bitter to me, so why do I envy them and wish to become their kind?

Even so, my inability to revert to human form saddens me to my core, and I still struggle to accept this fate of having to live the rest of my life as a dog. I have not stopped looking at the scroll.

A thought suddenly comes to me. As scary as it may seem, I must change into a python because that reverse spell, back to human form, is right below it!

What if the reverse spell does not work? I would rather be a dog than a python. I feel like tearing the scroll apart. It is made of skin. It won't be as easy as tearing paper, but chewing on it would sure give me satisfaction. But... this might be my only chance at regaining my human shape.

I start to memorize the spells, particularly the reverse spell. I also study the instructions that go with it, like which way to face while saying the words in my head. Then I perform the ritual, exactly as described. In seconds I feel my body going limp. My legs disappear and I am lying on my chest. From the corner of my eye, I glimpse the lower part of my body—a patterned serpent. Oh my God! I scare myself!

I start slithering across the garden and instinctively curl myself around a bush. Then the image of Mento comes to mind and I feel like heading towards the house, winding myself around him and squeezing the life out of him. I have to perform the reversing spell quickly, before I act on impulse.

Unfortunately the reversing spell will only work at the crack of dawn. I must spend what feels like hours willing myself to stay wound around the bush.

As I spot first light, I perform the rituals.

I open my eyes and realize I am lying in the garden. I try to get up, feeling my body with my hands as I go. But this is not my body. It is the emaciated body of some other man. Sure enough, hunger makes me feel faint. I have changed into someone else. I pick up the scroll, which has blown into the bush. I know there is a spell to change from one man to another, different man. I quickly memorize it and say the words.

The person I have changed into now must be loaded; I feel general well-being and ease. My body, as well as my mind, feels relaxed. But what I need is a spell that will turn me into *a particular person*. I start to wonder, while leisurely looking for such a spell, if I should change myself into the Prime Minister?

I study the instructions and perform the ritual. Finally! I only have to look at my hands and feet to recognize myself. Still, I can't wait to see myself in the mirror to be absolutely sure.

I need to get into the house, to get hold of a mirror and also to find some clothes. I have to do this before anyone wakes up.

I slip through the back door as I did, as a dog, only a couple of hours ago. All is quiet. Mento is still snoring.

I open the wardrobe that sits between the bedrooms. The full-length mirror on the door confirms that it is indeed me—a paler, leaner version. Thank God! I feel a lump in my throat. My joy is tempered only by the foul smell I notice coming from myself. I can't possibly take a shower. I spray myself with cologne I find in a drawer.

I see a couple of light suits stored here, probably awaiting the change of season. There is no underwear here, so I put on a pair of light, summery shorts, which hang loose on me, before I put on the shirt and the suit. I slip on a pair of light moccasins that I bought about two years ago. Why on earth do they still keep my stuff? Was Mento hoping to shrink a bit, to get into my expensive collection?

I exit by the same door with a spring in my step. I notice Mero is still asleep in the guard hut. Keleb must have left him one gratified man last night, for him to sleep so blissfully in his cot all night. As I open the gate to leave, I hear him making a startled noise in his sleep. I jog down the road that goes towards Dejach Wube neighbourhood.

I realize that I am still clutching the scroll. I slide it into the inside pocket of my slightly oversized jacket. I think about heading to my mother's house, but I change my mind. What if my mother gets a heart attack at seeing her son, whom she believes is dead? I need to be careful about this.

First things first—I need money. I wonder if my wife has changed the different accounts to her name? As a widow, she would be entitled to do so. If I start walking towards the National Theatre now, I will get to Awash Bank just as it opens.

I go straight to the Bank Manager's office when I get there. He is shocked to see me.

'But... how... Mr. Didimos... I, I heard... you were... dead.'

I employ peaceful gestures and kind words, and somehow I calm him down. I explain that, although people believed I was dead, I was only kidnapped by a gang of outlaws and kept in confinement without any means of communication.

'But if you were kidnapped, how come they didn't take your car? I heard it was found abandoned.'

'You are right,' I say soothingly. 'The gang was not after my money.'

'Were they a political group?'

'As you know, I don't get involved in politics,' I say, taking my seat. 'It would take a long time to explain everything. As you can see, the conditions they kept me in were quite rough. I haven't showered in a very long time... I stink!'

'I understand Mr. Didimos....' He takes out his wallet and pulls out a couple of hundred birr notes.

'No, no... I have lost my bank card... so I just want to ask if you can get me a new one, so I can withdraw money?' The Manager looks down for a few seconds. 'Please keep what I told you to yourself,' I caution him, while I await his reply.

'I understand,' he says, as he walks out. He comes back with a file in his hand and gives it to me. The first document shows that Ephrata has inherited the money as her husband, the account holder, was thought deceased and the children were still under age. Another document shows that she has officially changed the account to her name.

I stare at the Manager for some time and ask if he knows about the state of my other accounts, in other banks.

'I don't know about that,' he says, shaking his head. 'I was surprised at the way she rushed the process through. Not only that... within days I heard she had got remarried.'

'Can I ask you a favour?' I say, pressing the arms of the chair to get to my feet.

'No problem! I will happily do anything to help...'

'I need to take that money.'

'Of course you do... oh let me see....' He looks into his wallet again and gives me some more. I thank him for his kindness and remind him not to tell anyone about seeing me, or my situation. I then promise to call him and give him updates.

Although people will not easily recognize a person they believe to be dead, I stop to buy a black hat and a pair of dark glasses from a kiosk to disguise my appearance. I then jump into a taxi and visit the different banks I had accounts with. Every Bank Manager I meet is shocked at being face-to-face with a man they thought was dead. The answer is the same everywhere.

My hope is dwindling fast as I head to the last bank. As with the others, I calm the Manager of Zemen bank. I explain my situation and request a withdrawal of money.

'...if you lost your bankbook it is of course within your rights to ask for a new one. As we have not received a claim from your wife or received a court order regarding inheritance, we have a duty to give you your money. However, since this is an exceptional case, I need to consult with the legal team before I give my approval.'

'That's fine, sir,' I reply, as my hopes are revived once again.

'Anyway, fill out the form for getting a new book, and come back in two hours.'

I do as I am told, and leave the bank. I go to a nearby restaurant to grab some food and a coffee. Oh... how refreshing! I had forgotten how good traditionally brewed coffee tastes!

I return to the bank in high spirits. I arrive six minutes early for our appointment. The Manager welcomes me with a smile. He is with two other men, who I believe gave him counsel about my case. They stand up and greet me warmly. Once we are all seated, they formally compare my image with the images in my files. None of these people are strangers to me. In days past we have celebrated together lavishly, whenever I was granted a big loan for one of my various businesses. However, I understand the formalities—it is only appropriate for them to follow procedure.

After the verification process is over, I am told to bring a photo for my new book. I get back with the photo in about twenty-five minutes. Once I get hold of my new book, and am assured that I have sole control over it, I thank all of them and leave, charging them to keep the matter a secret.

Twenty-Eight

It has been two days since I managed to return to my original form. I have shaved. I also had a haircut, in another part of the city where I would be less likely to be recognized. I look better groomed generally, but I still have a sickly grey pallor to my skin.

With the money in my remaining account I have been able to buy everything I need. The house, car and clothes I manage to acquire testify to a reasonably respectable social status. On the inside however, the bone-deep pain I am experiencing over their betrayal is worsening by the hour.

I spend every free moment I have thinking about how I can avenge myself. Sleep and rest have proven elusive to me. Although I have not come across a definite plan of revenge, I have imagined various possibilities. The crumpled balls of paper on the floor of my hotel room testify to how much time I have spent in devising a plan. The plans I have come up with include:

- Take them both to a forest, tie them up in a clearing, and light a glorious bonfire to consume them alive.

- Take them to the wilderness and leave them there for beasts to feast upon.
- Hang Mento by his skin, from the same kind of hook he earned his nickname from.
- Change myself into a python, as I have done once before, wind myself around their deceiving bodies and crush the life out of them, then swallow their bodies whole.

As I jot down the last plan, I feel nauseous. I can't bring myself to even smell the damned couple, let alone swallow them.

Anyways, before I execute any one of my plans, there is something that needs to take priority. I need to escort my children to safety—they shouldn't witness me doing anything remotely evil. My mother's house is the safest place for them. This means I need to devise a plan to get my mother invite them to stay with her.

I want to call my mother. I dial her number a couple times and hang up before it even starts ringing. What if she faints on hearing my voice? How could she possibly bear to hear the sound of a son whom she thought was dead for almost a year?

I long to reach out to a trustworthy friend I can talk to about my predicament. I can't think of any. Where can one find a true friend in this age of fickleness? I think of all the friends I've had in the past. Not one had genuine purpose in life. Every one of them was motivated just by one thing—money.

The popular, Capitalist ideology of our modern culture has created a dog-eat-dog world. Where is the compassionate Ethiopian of the olden days? The Ethiopian, who was quick to lend a hand in times of crisis, will now gladly trade their dignity to gain a little extra money. Once Capitalism gets into the bloodstream of a society, it is neither easy to cure, nor satisfy.

I decide to end my dilemma and simply let my mother know that I am alive by calling her myself. It is much better for her to hear it from me than anyone else.

I dial the number.

'Hello...!' Hearing the sound of my mother's seasoned voice leaves me dumbfounded. I hang up the phone with trembling hands. I cannot bear to spend another sleepless night. So, I decide to go to my old house that night and do whatever has to be done. Hopefully my children will be asleep and will not have to witness anything ugly.

Twenty-Nine

The city is nodding off to sleep. As I head out of the Hilton and speed off towards my old home, the rain that arrived earlier in the evening is still pouring down. The deafening thunder is a blessing in disguise, I think, for what I have in mind.

As I approach the house, I note there isn't a single person around in the neighbourhood. I park the car in front of the gate and pull out a handgun I bought from an illegal dealer. I check that it is loaded and cock it, ready to fire. I slide it into my waistband and get out of the car.

I gently knock at the gate, hoping Mero will hear it. I hear him shuffling out of his hut, muttering curses as he comes to open the gate.

'Good evening Mero.'

He staggers back, and would fall over with shock if I didn't grab his arm in time to support him. I gather from his frightened look that he literally thinks I am a ghost. I help him through the gate and attempt to calm him. It isn't easy to convince him that I am actually alive and real, but I finally succeed.

'What a miracle! It's impossible...!' Mero keeps saying.

'Mero, it is a long story. I will tell you about it some other time,' I assure him.

'Oh... Dear... Oh my God! Yes, what would be impossible for the mighty Archangel Michael, who saved three young men from the furnace!' Mero holds his head with his two hands and won't let go.

'I was held prisoner by some bandits...' I have to lie again to put his mind at rest. This version doesn't seem to ease his worries. Now I realize that there is something else troubling him. He must be thinking about the man who is right now asleep with my wife.

'Are the children asleep?' I ask him.

'Yes, they are... But... Oh! My God...!'

'What is wrong Mero? Is there a problem?'

'Problem...? Yes, there are problems aplenty these days, sir...'

'I know what is worrying you. I have heard that my wife has married another man.'

His eyes bulge out in surprise. 'News travels fast! What else are folks good for except rumours, these days,' he says regretfully.

'Never mind, Mero. This is not a secret anyway.'

'You are right, sir. The entire neighbourhood is upset with them. They are acting like dogs in heat.'

'No Mero, they wouldn't have done this if they were dogs. Dogs are loyal creatures.'

'You are right, sir. It is just a figure of speech, to liken despicable behaviour to dogs. In truth, their loyalty is beyond that of men.'

'Are they both in?'

'Yes... sir.'

'Listen Mero. Pack your belongings. I have put down money on another house. We will go there as soon as I have done what I have come to do here.'

Mero looks confused. I guess he is worried about leaving Keleb behind.

'Tell Keleb to do the same. She is also coming with us.'

'Yes, sir,' he says brightly.

'Good... Now this is what you need to do. Go to my children's bedroom and gently wake them and tell them the good news tactfully. Tell them their father has just come back from a long journey. They will be less shocked if they hear about it before they see me.'

'Yes, sir. I will tell them gently. Don't worry. They will be fine. Leave it to me.'

'Wait Mero... Before that... first...' I am not sure of the sequence of events.

It looks like I am taking one cautious step at a time here. I have no clear picture of what the next step is yet. Each step pretty much depends on the previous one. Instinctive, uncertain moves. Such has been my personal journey, and my country's journey. A reversal, with the cart going before the horse, and the blind leading his guide. A life of nightmare and delusions...

Instinctively, I start walking towards the house. I pause for a second to check if this is really happening. Mero, also acting on instinct, grabs the metal bar he uses to prop open the gate and follows me, ready for battle. What else could it be?

What will the owner do if a robber forces his way into his house? What other alternative can he possibly have, apart from hitting the intruder where it hurts most and chasing him out? Involve the authorities? What for? The legal system is full of people like the robber himself. The adage, "a thief would rather exhaust their victim, than own up," confirms where we stand. This brings to mind an old verse:

> *Never say they loaded my mule*
> *Never say they took my wife*

> *For anything can happen,*
> *on the day your luck runs out.*

Someone must have gone through something similar to what I am going through to have coined such a verse.

'Mero!' I call out over my shoulder.

'Yes,' he replies nervously.

'I will wait for you in the garden. You go through the back door to the children's bedroom and do just as I have instructed you. Then, take them to your hut and tell them to wait there quietly, and return to me here. I will tell you the rest of the plan when you come back.'

After some time, I see Mero leading my children to his hut. He closes the door behind them and comes rushing to the garden.

'Were they very shocked when you told them the news?'

'Very much so, sir. But children are naïve, so their shock soon turned to excitement.'

'Were you quiet about it? Or do you think the master might have heard?'

'I swear he wouldn't have heard a thing.'

I walk in through the back door. Mero follows right behind me. I signal to him that he should stay quiet and wait in the living room. Once he takes his position, I burst into the master bedroom. The lights are still on.

The man looks alarmed. The wife lets out a shrill scream. They both start tugging at the bed sheets to cover their nakedness. When they finally realize who I am, they look utterly terrified. Mento tries to slip his hand under the pillow—I quickly draw my gun and point it at him, cautioning him not to make another move. I pull a chair out with my other hand and sit facing them.

They wait, apparently anxious to hear what I have to say. The fools don't seem to realize that words are precious. They chirp like birds, without weighing their words. Who can tell them that such precious treasure should not be wasted on damned traitors like them?

If I say to them, 'You have betrayed me, not once or twice, but multiple times. Can you not betray me enough?' what can they reply? I know that no scrap of truth can be found in this couple's materialistic mind, or their sullied consciences. So, I won't utter a word, neither do I want them to make even a squeak.

Words are like precious stones. They are like ore; with refinement it can be used either to cure people of their maladies, or to make bullets. Similarly words are precious. They are like the master key that opens the door to all things, good or bad.

Words should not be used inappropriately. One has to be discerning about when and how, or if it is wise to use them at all. Words can change men into dogs, but they can also restore their humanity. Words can bring about good things, but they can also take them away. Words can simply extinguish the light, but they can also illuminate darkness. They can enrich people's lives, or they can impoverish them. My tongue and lips will be preserved from uttering inappropriate words. I know the power of words from first-hand experience. Words have changed me into a dog, but they have also restored me again, to become human.

The traitors in front of me, and their kind, not only use words wrongly but also relationships. They use their bodies inappropriately. They use freedom wrongly. They use their position, whether inferior or superior, wrongly. They use their knowledge, as well as their ignorance, wrongly. They use technology wrongly. They use their kinship and identity wrongly. They use political ideology wrongly. They even use their religion wrongly.

They think they are alive just because they breathe and move around, but in actual fact they are zombies.

More than this; these dead souls will do anything to bury those who are alive and clear-headed.

I feel the urge to cast a magic spell and shift myself into a serpent's form. For the umpteenth time, I imagine coiling around them and crushing them to death. But, those mystic words are too important to waste on creatures who've damned themselves.

I sit there for a long time and stare at them. I can sense their fear, they sweat profusely, but they are too scared to even squirm. I wonder if they at all manage to reflect on what they have done in life. I bet they can't recall a single great deed they have accomplished in their dreadful lives. That should prompt them to realize for the first time how empty they are.

There is no punishment greater than this—the echoing announcement in one's own mind that he or she is nothing. If I allow them to restore to me what they have robbed and let them go free, would that be a great gift? What if I leave everything as it is and walk away? Would they then consider me a fool? Which of these two options would break their hearts?

Right now, everything they possess, including their lives, is in my hands to do with as I please. To end everything is as easy as aiming the gun to their heads and pulling the trigger. I aim it straight at their heads for a long time. But I don't see a life worth taking. Shooting at an empty vessel, just like breaking an empty bottle. Maybe if I do something they would never dream of doing if they were in my shoes—that might leave a lasting impression in their empty heads.

What if I leave them be? What if I forgive them? Would they understand how much harm they have caused me? I guess, as long as I do something that my conscience can accept, it won't matter if they learn from it or not.

'Do you mind if I forgive you?' I ask aloud, before I make a conscious decision to speak. Their eyes bulge out even more.

'The only two things I want from this house are my children and my books. I know you don't care for either of them. But I want them more than you ever cared for any of these material possessions you would kill for.'

Their lips seem to be sealed. The way they sit there frozen, they look like they have turned into statues. I get up and leave the room. I tell Mero and Keleb to load my books in the car, and run to the guard's hut to see my children. As I open the door, my heart quivers upon seeing both my children's faces awash with tears. I bend down to receive them as they both rush towards me for a hug. We can't let go of each other, neither can we stop our tears. Inhaling their sweet scent that I so longed for is pure bliss.

Slowly, we head to our new home. It seems the children don't want to be parted from me for a single moment. I hope they will grow up to be good people. Who can live without hope? I see all my hopes reflected in their eyes, bright with joy.

Scroll of Honour

The publication of this book was made possible by the following supporters on Unbound:

ADEPTS

Brook Bayuh • Paul Griffiths • Cat Heeley • Jack Page • Jackie Morris
M M • Matt Curran • Esme Pears • W Tom Lawrie • Michael O'Neil

NOVICES

John Mitchinson • Azi Bayuh • Mig Bogale • Jane Wilson-Howarth
Lydia Mengistu • Carolyn Sunners • Claire Allen • Lisa Bird
Megan McCormick • Adrian Oliver • Mary Jordan-Smith • Katrina
Moseley • Joanne Smith • David Hebblethwaite • Joy Walsh • Koen
Koggel • Richard Hughes • Jesús Martín Sánchez • Neil Harrison
Tanya Peixoto • Andrea Barlien • Paul Fulcher • Brad Bone
Luciana Miranda • Thom Josephson • Hannah Piekarz • Cam Field

Acknowledgements

African language fiction does not travel easily beyond its national borders because of language barriers. It is an honour to enable *The Lost Spell* to cross beyond Ethiopian borders through my translation.

Thank you David and Ping, for helping my translation find its destination. My heartfelt thanks go to my husband Ian Attfield and Jayne Harthan for their valuable input, and Agnes Gautier for directing me to the right people.

Bethlehem Attfield, 2022

PhD Research Student,

University of Birmingham, Modern Languages Dept.

David and Ping Henningham would also like to thank
Sophie O'Neill, Jane Pike and Inpress Books.
Arts Council England literature team.
John Mitchinson and Unbound.

About the Author

Yismake Worku is an Ethiopian novelist and poet.

He was just 22 when his debut novel *Dertogada* became a bestseller.

He has published 12 books in Amharic.

Bethlehem Attfield is an Amharic-English literary translator and author.

She was born in Addis Ababa, where she studied English language and literature. In 1998, she left for Britain to study for a Masters degree.

Attfield's translation *Requiem For Potatoes* by Adam Reta, with original songs, was published as an audiobook in 2020. She also founded the Ethiopian Literary Translators Network.

She is currently undertaking a practice-based PhD at Birmingham University and hosting a YouTube podcast: *Journey to Ethiopia with Story*.

Henningham Family Press

Since 2006, we have been a microbrewery for books.

Our ingenious handmade editions can be found in the V&A, Tate, National Galleries Scotland, National Poetry Library and Stanford University.

Our Performance Publishing shows compress the creation of printed matter into hectic live events.

Now our Fiction brings you authors who are re-inventing the conventions of Modern writing.

HENNINGHAM
FAMILY
PRESS